GIRLS CAN VLOG

Jazzy Jessie

'Pitch-perfect fiction for the new digital generation' *Lancashire Evening Post*

'Funny and inspirational story about the world of vlogging' *Bookseller*

'Warm, funny, and perfect for the Zoella generation, this series is bang on trend and sure to be a hit' The Mile Long Bookshelf

'A really fun read . . . sends out a really positive message that social networking can be a powerful force for good when it's supported by a healthy dose of interaction in the real world' Sugarscape

'Makes great reading for anyone who wants to give vlogging a go' *Week Junior*

'The story itself is wonderful, funny and descriptive – so much so that I read the whole thing in one day!' Ella, age 11, a Lovereading4kids.co.uk Reader Review Panel member

'I really enjoyed this funny book' Miyah, age 10, a Lovereading4kids.co.uk Reader Review Panel member

'A brilliant story about friends, vlogging and adorable animals!' Sidney, age 12, a Lovereading4kids.co.uk Reader Review Panel member

Books by Emma Moss

The Girls Can Vlog series

Lucy Locket: Online Disaster

Amazing Abby: Drama Queen

Hashtag Hermione: Wipeout!

Jazzy Jessie: Going for Gold

Emma Moss

GIRLS CAN VLOG

Jazzy Jessie
Going for Gold

MACMILLAN CHILDREN'S BOOKS

First published 2017 by Macmillan Children's Books
an imprint of Pan Macmillan
20 New Wharf Road, London N1 9RR
Associated companies throughout the world
www.panmacmillan.com

ISBN 978-1-5098-1742-9

Based on an original concept by Ingrid Selberg
Copyright © Ingrid Selberg Consulting Limited and Emma Young 2017

1 3 5 7 9 8 6 4 2

A CIP catalogue record for this book is available from
the British Library.

Typeset by Nigel Hazle
Printed and bound by CPI Group (UK) Ltd, Croydon CR0 4YY

To all good friends

Chapter One

TO-DO LIST

1. April Fool's Day is coming – time to brainstorm some A+ . . . Need to get my girls and get 'em good, hahaha. Something food related?? *And* capture it all on camera, obv!

2. More gymnastics: Put in SERIOUS hours on the beam . . . Olympics, here I come!

3. Catch up with my YouTube watching. **Wish I had my own MacBook instead of my dad's ancient laptop**

4. Buy ingredients for pranks.

5. Babysit Max – Thursday.
6. Easter prep: Make a list of fave choc for Mum and Dad and leave it hanging around. Never too old for the Easter bunny!!

Jessie sat on the bus home from Abby's house, playing *Candy Crush* on her phone and chewing on a jelly worm. After what had felt like an eternity, her braces had finally been removed a couple of weeks earlier and, as well as loving her new smile, she was having the best time rediscovering her favourite gummy sweets, even though the dentist had told her to go easy on them.

'Hi, doggy!' she said cheerfully to the miniature dachshund who had got on the bus with his owner, sniffed her trainers, and settled down on her right foot. 'I don't mind,' she replied as the owner apologized. 'I've just been playing football with my friend's dog; he can probably smell him on me!'

She'd been at Abby's house with Lucy and Hermione for their regular after-school Girls Can Vlog meeting. On top of the usual business of discussing content and brainstorming ideas for future videos, Abby had been keen to talk about their preparation for SummerTube. There were only a few months to go until the big YouTube convention, and Abby said they needed to take the channel to the 'next level' before then. Whatever that meant.

Jessie had leaped at the chance to give Weenie the pug a runaround in the garden and take a moment's peace from the intensely businesslike atmosphere of Abby's room. She loved their vlogging club, but, honestly, sometimes it felt more like a full-time job than a hobby!

'Sorry, little guy – this is my stop,' she said, jumping up and ringing the bell, shaking the dachshund gently off her foot.

Lucy had suggested that they film an April Fool's Day prank for the channel, as 1st April was coming up, and they'd all agreed to think of ideas . . . but secretly Jessie had her own plans. *Oh yeah*, she mused as she stepped off the bus. *I'm gonna trick them all myself. They won't be expecting a solo prank – genius!*

Letting herself into her house five minutes later, she was mildly surprised to see that her parents were both in the kitchen: Mum stirring something on the hob, and Dad carrying a sleepy Max off to bed. Because of their differing work schedules, it was rare for them to be at home together during the week.

'Goodnight, Maxy!' she called. Her little brother waved as he was carted off to his room. 'Mum, I'm starving. What's cooking?'

'Pasta and pesto,' said her mum, passing her some parmesan to grate. 'How was your meeting?'

Jessie grabbed the cheese grater. 'Good! Abby's in an extra-bubbly mood these days – I think it's because Dakota and Ben have officially broken up.'

'Ah! That Abby – always chasing after boys!' Mrs Dunbar laughed. She eyed the rapidly growing pile of cheese. 'OK, that's enough, even for you lot. Call your brothers.'

A few minutes later the family – minus Max – sat down around the table.

'I've decided to prank the girls,' said Jessie, filling her glass with juice. 'I need something really good, for April Fool's Day. Any ideas? Something totally different to anything I've done before.' She glanced at Jake hopefully. Her middle brother loved pranks almost as much as she did, and they were always comparing notes on the funniest new YouTubers.

'Yes!' said Jake eagerly, shovelling pasta spirals into his mouth. 'I'm sooo glad you asked. Today I saw this thing you can do with a thermos full of soup—'

'Actually, before we get on to that,' interrupted Jessie's mum, glancing over at her husband, 'there's something we all need to talk about . . .' She put her fork down, and the expression on her face worried Jessie.

'What?' asked Leon stroppily. He glanced towards the

living room. 'My match starts in ten minutes, so this had better be quick.'

Jessie kicked him. He was two years older than her, so why did *she* always have to keep *him* in line?

'Mum's trying to tell us something,' she hissed. 'I think it's important.'

'Whatever, Miss Butter Wouldn't Melt. I'm not the one who got sent home from my school ski trip for underage drinking,' drawled Leon.

Jake looked up, surprised. 'Jessie was drinking on that trip? Actual alcohol?'

'No!' squealed Jessie. 'Jeez, Leon!' It was still a sore subject – having to miss the last few days of snowboarding in France had been so depressingly awful. 'That was all a misunderstanding, Dakota set me up. Which Leon KNOWS. He's just being an idiot.' She glared at him across the table.

'Yes, that's enough, Leon,' said her mum. 'Anyway, kids, we have some news. Your father's job . . .' She stopped. 'Do you want to explain, love?'

Her dad nodded and cleared his throat. 'Guys, I don't want you to worry, OK? But the company's not been doing brilliantly for a while, and well – long story short – I am now . . . technically . . . without a job.'

Jessie gasped and exchanged looks with her brothers.

'There's no need to panic,' he continued. 'Your mum and I have known about this for a while now and we've made some plans for how to deal with the situation before I find a new role.'

'I'm so sorry, Dad,' said Jessie, the pasta settling like a rock in her stomach. For as long as she could remember, her father had always loved his job in IT. Despite the long hours in the office, he seemed to thrive on the pressure. She gave him a hopeful smile. 'Is it definitely a done deal?'

'Yes, sweetie.' He sighed. 'Not the best timing, but your mum's going to do extra shifts at the hospital, and—'

'How can Mum do any *more* shifts?' interrupted Jake sulkily. 'She's hardly ever here as it is.'

'Enough, Jakey!' said their mum. 'I can do a

bit more now that your dad will be around to take care of things at home. He's keen to do more cooking, for one thing.'

'Oh no,' Leon mumbled. 'Please no haggis. It literally makes me vom.'

Their father was Scottish and occasionally liked to experiment with the cuisine of his birthplace, with varying degrees of success.

As her brothers complained, Jessie was still processing the news. Suddenly something occurred to her and she sat up straight in her seat.

'But you had to pay extra for me to come home from the ski trip early,' she wailed at her parents. 'AND I've just had my room redone! That must have been expensive. Those new lights, the painting . . .'

'Well, don't feel too guilty,' said her dad. 'You've actually reminded me of the next thing we need to tell you about.'

'Is it as depressing as the last thing?' grumbled Leon, looking at his phone.

'No – well, it's another big change . . . but hopefully we can all be open-minded about it.' He paused. 'We're getting a lodger. To help with the bills.'

There was silence.

'Like, someone who lives in our house? A complete stranger?' asked Jake nervously.

'Someone we know nothing about, who might murder us in our beds?' added Leon, waggling his eyebrows dramatically.

Jessie rolled her eyes. 'Let's hope so, in your case. But, uh, Dad – where is this person supposed to go? We don't have a spare room.'

'Well, darling – remember you just mentioned the work we did in your bedroom?' said her mother tentatively.

'Yeah . . . ?' Jessie took a sip of juice.

'It makes sense for that to be the room we rent out. It's by far the most modern and welcoming.'

Leon burst out laughing as Jessie spat out her drink.

'My actual bedroom? What! But where would I go?'

'As it's probably only going to be for a few months, we thought it might be fun for you to share with Maxy,' said her mum lightly. 'His nursery's far too big for him, especially once you tidy away all the toys. There's acres of space.' She didn't quite meet Jessie's eyes.

'Oh man – this is too good,' crowed Leon.

Jessie glared at him and stood up, furiously pushing back her chair.

'But where is all my stuff supposed to go? And – wait – how can I do any filming with Max in there crying his eyes out?' she said, pacing around the kitchen. 'Or gym practice? Jeez! Why can't Leon be the one to share? He has zero hobbies – unless you count lying around playing *Minecraft*.'

'Jessie, sit down, love,' said her father, looking at her anxiously. 'Max spends a lot of time down here or at nursery. And there's plenty of storage room in those cupboards.'

'I promise you'll have some time to yourself,' added

her mum. 'We understand that you need plenty of your own space.'

'Why? It's not like she has a boyfriend,' drawled Leon.

Jessie sat down abruptly, the reality of the situation hitting her. 'Do we even know who this lodger person is?' she asked grumpily.

'Yes, your mum and I have met her via a student letting agency,' said her father. 'Her name is Gabriella, she's from Mexico, and she's over here studying chemistry. She seems very studious; I'm sure she'll spend a lot of time revising in her room.'

'Is she fit?' asked Leon, prompting Jake to wolf-whistle. 'How old is she?'

'Ugh, why are you so gross, Leon!' cried Jessie.

Noticing the despairing looks on her parents' faces, she was suddenly struck by pity for both of them. She decided to pull herself together. It was clear her stupid brothers weren't going to be responsible about this, so someone had to be.

'OK, fine. When do I have to move my stuff?'

21:38

Jessie: SOS GUYS – THE WORST HAS HAPPENED!

21:45

Lucy: What???

21:56

Hermione: RU OK? x

21:59

Abby: Spill!

22:02

Jessie: My dad lost his job and we're getting a LODGER.

22:02

Jessie: WHO IS TAKING OVER MY ROOM ☹

22:04

Lucy: And you have to share with them??

22:04

Jessie: Lol no. With MAX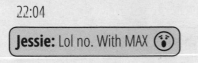

22:07

Hermione: Woah! That's rough!

22:09

Jessie: Worst bit is – she's coming NEXT WEEK.

22:09

Jessie: I have to move my stuff this WEEKEND.

22:11

Abby: Wow. We can help . . . I'm great at interiors!!

22:14

Lucy: Yeah happy to help xxxx

22:17

Hermione: Me too.

22:18

Jessie: You guys are the best. Bring snacks!! xox

VLOG 1

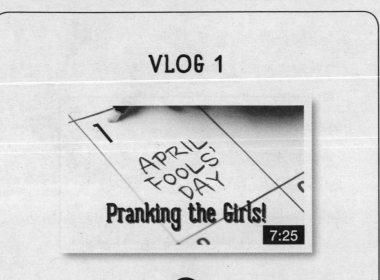

Pranking the Girls!

7:25

FADE IN: JESSIE'S KITCHEN.

JESSIE is at the counter in a polka-dot apron.

JESSIE

Hi, guys! So have you checked your calendars recently? That's right – it's nearly time for APRIL FOOL'S DAY! The girls think we're filming an April Fool video here tomorrow, but what they DON'T know is that I'm going to prank them first. It's time for a surprise picnic that they'll never forget! I'm preparing some delicious 'treats', like these doughnuts drenched with talcum

powder that looks like icing sugar. I'll put them in an old Krispy Kreme box to help mislead them. Mwahaha!

MONTAGE: Sped-up footage of JESSIE sprinkling doughnuts with powder and putting them in box.

JESSIE
(CONTINUED)

Then I'm making this amazing-looking cake, which is two kitchen sponges covered with whipped cream, then drizzled with chocolate sauce, and finally some cake sprinkles.

MONTAGE: JESSIE covering the sponges with whipped cream from spray can and decorating them.

JESSIE (CONTINUED)

OMG – this looks perfect! No one would ever guess what's really inside. OK, now I've got to get this stuff to the park, then make some calls. Stay tuned . . .

FADE TO: THE PARK.

In the park with picnic spread out on blanket on ground, JESSIE is holding the camera facing her.

JESSIE (CONTINUED)

(on phone)

Hey, Lucy! Listen, I really need your help. I'm in the park by the swings and I've just found an injured bird. It must have fallen out of its nest. I don't know what to do?! Pleeeease come now!

(grinning)

You can? Thank you sooo much. See you soon! Byeee.

JESSIE dials again.

JESSIE (CONTINUED)

(on phone)

Hey, Abs! You busy? I could really use your help with choosing

an outfit for this party I'm going to next weekend. Could you

meet me in the park where I'm minding Maxy until Leon

comes, and then we could go to the shops from here? OK,

great! I'm by the swings . . . See ya!

JESSIE hangs up the phone and looks into the camera.

JESSIE (CONTINUED)

(gleeful)

Two down and one to go . . .

JESSIE dials phone.

JESSIE (CONTINUED)

Hi, Hermione! Can you do me a favour? Would you listen to

me practise my report for English and tell me honestly what you think? I'm so nervous about it. Really? Well, now would be good. I'm in the park by the swings babysitting Maxy. OK, amazing. I'll see you soon! Byee!

JESSIE hangs up.

JESSIE (CONTINUED)

(to camera)

I can't wait to see what happens when they all turn up and sit down to my DELICIOUS picnic! I'm off to hide behind the cafe, where they won't be able to see me.

CUT TO: Handheld footage – through some tree leaves, we see LUCY rushing over to the swings.

LUCY

(calling out)

Jessie! Jessie! Where are you?! Where's the b-bird? Oh, Abs, what are you d-doing here?

ABBY walks into shot.

ABBY

I'm supposed to be meeting Jessie. She wanted me to meet her here to go shopping. Where is she?

LUCY

Well, she called me too to come help r-rescue a wounded bird. Ooh, just got a text from her.

LUCY takes out her phone and reads.

LUCY (CONTINUED)

(reading aloud)

SURPRISE! Gone to loo – see ya soon.

Enjoy the picnic I've laid out for you! Jess.

ABBY

That's weird! Never mind, let's tuck into some doughnuts while

we wait for her. Oh, look, here comes Hermione!

HERMIONE walks into shot.

HERMIONE

What are you guys doing here? I'm supposed to be meeting

Jess . . .

LUCY

Us too. But she's left us a p-picnic . . . It must be a surprise!

Fancy a doughnut or some c-cake?

JESSIE turns the camera around and we see her laughing silently.
Camera turns back to the girls.

LUCY cuts a piece of cake while ABBY picks up doughnut and

takes a big bite. One chew and she spits it out in disgust.

ABBY

YUCK! That's totally disgusting! UGH. What *is* it?

(she hands it to HERMIONE)

HERMIONE

I don't think that's sugar on top . . . it smells

like talcum powder!

LUCY squeals, spitting out a mouthful of sponge.

LUCY

This c-cake isn't right either!

JESSIE, still filming, runs out from behind trees.

JESSIE

APRIL FOOL! HAHAHA! GOTCHA!

LUCY

(laughing)

W-what is wrong with you?!

ABBY

Queen of Pranks!

They all push her into the fake cake.

JESSIE gets up, wiping the icing off her face.

JESSIE

That was such a hoot. Guys – I got you some real

doughnuts to say sorry . . .

JESSIE gives the girls a box of Krispy Kremes and turns to the camera.

JESSIE (CONTINUED)

I'm such a bad friend, ha ha! But they love me anyway. Give us a thumbs-up below if you enjoyed this video, and let me know if you've played a prank for April Fool's Day. Byeee!

FADE OUT.

Views: 2,878

Subscribers: 9,430

Comments:

MagicMorgan: Jessie you're evil! Love it!

PrankingsteinJosh: We need to try that doughnut prank!

SassySays: LOVE IT. ♥♥♥ Also, you guys are nearly at 10k!! xx

billythekid: A bird fell from the tree?! Can't believe you fell for that ha ha!

natalie_blogs: Abby where is your top from in this video?

Amazing_Abby_xxx: Topshop sale! Go go go x

Jakethechamp: Nice one sis!

***jazzyjessie*:** Thanks bro :)

(scroll down to see 17 more comments)

Chapter Two

'Ah, Jessie, glad you could join us!'

'Hi, Laila,' gasped Jessie as she dashed into the hall and stood near one of the free mats in the front row. 'Sorry I'm late!' She'd gone halfway home after school before remembering that her dad was looking after Max and she was free to go to the sports centre for gymnastics. The sessions were on a pay-as-you-go basis, and she only came when she could make it, but she knew her coach, Laila, wanted her to commit to coming more regularly. The bus ride only took about ten minutes from the stop outside school, and her mum had offered to pay for more sessions in exchange for Jessie giving up her room.

The young coach smiled at her. 'Don't worry. I'm just glad you made it. Your attendance hasn't been, shall we say, *easy to predict* lately.'

Jessie squirmed. 'I know, I know.' She shoved her braids into a scrunchie to make a topknot. 'Things have changed at home though, and basically I'm off the hook with babysitting my little brother.' She grinned hopefully. 'So I'm planning to come here for both sessions every week now, if that's OK?'

Laila clapped her hands together. 'If it's OK?! Jess – it's music to my ears! As you know, I really think you've got some potential, but the only way we're going to draw it out of you is with regular practice.'

Jessie's heart lifted at the praise. Their PE teacher at school, Mr Evans, frequently complimented her, but he encouraged *all* of his students, even those who could barely manage a forward roll. If Laila, a specialized coach, thought Jessie was something special, then maybe she *did* actually have some talent. She'd always loved gymnastics with a passion and had done pretty well in a few small competitions when she was younger, but she'd been distracted with other things over the last two years.

Laila turned and addressed the other girls in the room. 'OK, gang. Today we're going to be trying some pairs work, so it's great that Jessie has made it, because now we're a nice even number. Anya, come and join Jessie over here.'

A girl who Jessie hadn't seen before came over to stand at the neighbouring mat.

'Hi, I'm Anya,' she said, her clear blue eyes staring at Jessie. Her hair was scraped into a severe bun fixed with dozens of kirby grips so that not a single strand could escape. 'Why were you late?' she demanded.

Jessie bristled, adjusting the strap of her leotard. How was it any of this girl's business? 'Er, family stuff,' she replied. 'Anyway, I'm here now! How old are you?'

Anya was a head shorter than Jessie, though she stood with a very straight back, making her seem taller.

'Fourteen. I just moved here from Poland.'

'Oh, really? How come?' said Jessie, intrigued.

That explained the unfamiliar accent. But Anya seemed to have switched off. Her gaze had returned to Laila, who started taking them through their warm-up exercises.

'You're the same age as me,' Jessie whispered as they jogged on the spot.

But again, there was no response. Anya was concentrating hard, eyes to the front of the room, as if nothing in the world could distract her.

Weird, thought Jessie. *Maybe she's just shy?*

Definitely not shy! concluded Jessie fifty minutes later, wiping a bead of sweat from her forehead. They'd been working on a two-person forward roll, which always looked easy on gymnastics videos, but was frustratingly difficult to get right in real life. She kept losing hold of Anya's ankles. But Anya was a strong, precise gymnast, and she'd obviously trained a lot. She barked instructions at Jessie, at one point rushing over to her bag to get a notebook and draw a diagram.

'Very nice,' said Laila, looking on as they executed their best one yet. 'Controlled and graceful. You guys make quite the team –' she raised her voice – 'which is more than can be said for some of the other slackers around here!' Jessie looked around at the other pairs, several of whom had given up and were chatting on their mats, or were still trying, but dissolving into giggles every time the manoeuvre went wrong, collapsing helplessly on to the ground.

'OK, everyone – that's enough. Stop chatting and let's start our cool-down,' said Laila, much to Jessie's relief. She usually had bags of energy, but she felt absolutely drained by Anya's boot-camp training style.

They returned to their mats, and Laila led them through their stretches.

'My old partner in Poland was shorter,' Anya muttered to Jessie, reaching an arm down her back and pushing on her elbow to stretch it. 'It's taking some adjustment to work with someone of your height.' She sighed impatiently.

'Jeez, sorry for being tall!' Jessie chuckled. 'Not much I can do about it, I'm afraid!'

Anya rolled her eyes, releasing her arm. 'Of course you can't. And you are very flexible, which is good. All is not lost.'

'OK, well that's something!' said Jessie, with a bemused grin. This girl baffled her – she'd never seen someone take an after-school club so seriously. She sounded about forty!

'Pairs come in all shapes and sizes,' remarked Laila as they cleared up their mats. 'You don't have to look identical, and today was a great start. In fact, I'm wondering if we have time to enter you two into the under-fifteens pairs competition in a few months' time. Intermediate category.'

'Intermediate? But this was my first experience of pairs!' cried Jessie. 'I'm a total beginner.'

'She's not ready,' agreed Anya curtly.

Jessie flinched. 'OK, and what are you – an Olympic medallist I somehow haven't heard of?'

Anya almost cracked a smile. 'Not quite. But I made the under-fifteens quarter-finals in Poland last year.'

'Wow!' said Jessie, impressed despite herself. 'Was that with your perfectly sized partner?' she added sarcastically.

'Yes.' Anya glanced at Jessie. 'She's not perfect in every way though; she was terribly grumpy some of the time. And bossy. Very bossy.'

Jessie raised her eyebrows. 'Can't imagine what that must have been like.'

Laila laughed. 'Seems you two have a natural chemistry. Jessie, I know you're new to this, but let me find out some more details about the competition and then we can talk again at the next session.' She made a note on her clipboard, then tapped her pen thoughtfully. 'You said you had more time to practise now, and we've got weeks before the competition . . . I think it could really work.'

Jessie's heart beat a little faster as she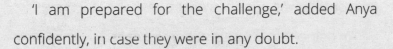
imagined medal tables, rows of judges and a
special leotard with matching scrunchie. 'OK,' she
shrugged. It seemed like a different planet and a million
miles away from anything she'd ever done before. 'I
think you're both insane though.'

'I am prepared for the challenge,' added Anya
confidently, in case they were in any doubt.

In the changing room, Jessie removed her practice shorts
and threw her tracksuit bottoms and T-shirt on over her
leotard. She didn't have time to change properly – she
only had an hour to get home and do that evening's
filming before dinner. Apparently Dad was making his
new speciality, whatever that was, and she'd promised
to clear away her camera stuff by Maxy's bedtime. She
was filming a room tour of her and Max's new 'shared
space', and his stuff was all over the floor, despite the
girls' best efforts to help her sort it out.

Maybe she'd leave it messy though, in the name of

honesty. All her favourite YouTubers were making their videos more 'real' at the moment – to show their viewers that nobody's life was that perfect in reality.

'See ya next time,' she said to Anya. 'Gotta dash!'

'Why in such a hurry?' asked the girl curiously, brushing out her ash-blonde hair, which was surprisingly long once it was out of its neat bun.

'I'm doing some filming at home,' replied  Jessie. 'Loads to prepare.'

'Filming of your gymnastics?'

'No – of my room.'

Anya looked blank, so Jessie explained further.

'Do you know what a room tour is? Like, on YouTube?'

Anya shrugged. 'I don't really watch YouTube apart from gymnastics. Do you put your own videos on there?'

'Yeah – I do it with my friends,' said Jessie. She loved talking about Girls Can Vlog to new people. 'We film all sorts of things, and a room tour shows the viewers our bedrooms and the kind of stuff we have in there, you know. I've had to move in with my little brother and all his toys, so this video is going to be an absolute MESS – usually people make their rooms look nice! But the girls thought it would be fun.'

'Doesn't sound like you'll have much space to practise your gymnastics in this room,' said Anya, a note of concern in her voice.

Jessie could tell Anya wasn't that interested in the whole vlogging thing. 'I'll work it out, don't worry! Anyway, we haven't committed to anything yet – that competition might not happen. See ya next time!' Jessie grabbed her bag and ran off with a wave. *And I thought I was gymnastics obsessed! Anya needs to chill!*

VLOG 2

Room Tour – Sharing with My Little Brother! 9:03

FADE IN: MAXY AND JESSIE'S BEDROOM.

One half has a neatly made single bed with a turquoise zebra-striped duvet covering it and a small wardrobe in the corner. The wall is bedecked with chilli-pepper-shaped fairy lights, a Beth Tweddle poster, a bedside table cluttered with a small mirror, alarm clock, sports magazines and a phone.

The other half is a complete mess, with an unmade child-sized bed half covered with a Star Wars duvet, a nightlight, and toys strewn all over the floor.

JESSIE is filming herself in the tiny mirror.

JESSIE

Hi, everyone! So I thought I'd give you an updated room tour . . . now that I've had to surrender my amazing room – sigh – to share with my baby brother Maxy. We've taken in a lodger, and guess who lost her room!
(makes a shocked face)
Hopefully it won't last forever.

JESSIE pans over the room.

JESSIE (CONTINUED)

So, you can see my side has a lot of my stuff from my old bedroom, but now it's really squished together. Most of all I miss my big wardrobe – I just have sooo little room for my stuff! The only good thing is that it's forcing me to keep things very tidy!

But over on Maxy's side it looks like a tornado has swept through! No matter how often I help him put away his toys, we always end up with Lego and action figures all over the floor. The worst thing is when Maxy gets into my stuff. Yesterday he totally destroyed the eyeshadow palette that Abs gave me for Christmas, which I'd left out on my bed.

JESSIE turns the camera back to her to pull a sad face.

JESSIE (CONTINUED)

It's the first one I've ever had. She was trying to get me to experiment with all the different colours. I guess Maxy experimented for me – all over my duvet.

JESSIE shows the now multicoloured duvet cover.

JESSIE (CONTINUED)
What I really miss is not having the space to practise my gymnastics.

JESSIE sets the camera down, does a cartwheel and crashes into her bed. She picks the camera up again.

JESSIE (CONTINUED)
Whoops! Anyway, I've decided to make gymnastics more of a priority from now on. I'm going to have to work really hard to make the grade . . . if any of you do gymnastics, leave me a comment and let me know!

MAX rushes into the room. JESSIE scoops him up.

JESSIE (CONTINUED)

Hey, Maxy! Shall we go see what Leon and Jake are up to?

(to camera)

Time to wrap this up! Give us a thumbs-up if you liked this

vlog. Bye!

FADE OUT.

Views: 2,540

Subscribers: 10,023

Comments:

SassySays: 10k subscribers!!

jazzyjessie: Woo-hoo! 🎉

queen_dakota: You must be bribing people with sub for

subs . . .

girlscanvlogfan: I don't have to share but my room is tiny!

Easier to clean at least ;)

GabsDoesGym: Meeee! 👍 I love gymnastics! I'm always

looking for places to practise too . . .

xxrainbowxx: RIP your eyeshadow palette :(

StephSaysHi: I share with my sister but I kinda like it as I can steal her clothes!

PrankingsteinJosh: Beth Tweddle rules 👍

(scroll down to see 14 more comments)

Chapter Three

'To ten thousand subscribers . . . and, more importantly, the Easter holidays!' Two glasses of Coke, one of Fanta and one of Sprite clinked together as the members of Girls Can Vlog crowded around a table in their beloved Pizza Planet.

'FIIIINALLY!' said Abby in a long-suffering tone. 'This term has dragged on forever. Although I'm not sure how much fun I can have over the holidays – my mum is making me do two hours a day with my stupid new tutor. Hashtag *help*! When am I meant to vlog, or go on dates, or do *anything*?'

The girls burst out laughing at her tragic expression.

Abby and schoolwork had never exactly been a match made in heaven.

'Here we go, ladies,' announced the waitress, setting two extra-large Comet Cheese Feast pizzas on to the table, one with added jalapeño peppers.

'Hello, beautiful,' said Jessie, happily addressing the spicy pizza – her all-time favourite. She reached for a slice and took a huge bite. 'Don't worry, Abs,' she continued, her mouth full of hot stringy cheese. 'It's only two hours a day. I've got stuff to do too, for gym. I still haven't decided whether to enter that pairs competition.'

Laila had looked into the entry requirements and told Jessie that morning that she would be ready, as long as she put in enough training time with Anya to allow them to learn some new skills.

'Y-you should totally g-go for it,' said Lucy, and Hermione nodded in agreement. 'What have you got to lose?'

Jessie grinned. 'What, apart from my self-respect, the

respect of Anya, and the possibility of doing too much training and pulling a Hermione?'

'Hey!' Hermione flinched. 'What's "pulling a Hermione"?!'

'We've been saying it for ages,' said Jessie cheerfully. 'Well, since your skiing accident, obvs. To describe someone injuring themselves in a noticeable way.'

Hermione looked blank, so Jessie carried on.

'Like, the other day, Abby tripped up the stairs at school and got a nosebleed, and Lucy said, "Wow, way to pull a Hermione!"'

Hermione glanced accusingly at Lucy, who put down her pizza slice. 'I didn't invent it, H, I p-promise!' she insisted.

Jessie thought of another example. 'And then a couple of weeks ago, when Abby heard that Ben had sprained his ankle playing football, she said—'

'OK, OK – I think she gets it,' said Abby, giggling, as Hermione rolled her eyes and then thrust out her left leg from under the table.

'Do I have to remind you, the cast came off ages ago! And that was my first time skiing!'

Jessie coughed, trying not to laugh. She knew her sense of humour sometimes went a bit too far and she hadn't meant to upset Hermione. 'Sorry, H – we're only teasing. Anyway, so yeah, that gymnastics competition means loads of stress. Plus try practising floor work at my place at the moment – it's a total madhouse. Anya wants me to do twenty hours a week. As if!'

Lucy raised an eyebrow. 'This Anya sounds incredibly p-pushy.'

'She's actually OK,' said Jessie loyally. 'I'll have to introduce you guys some time. She's just very – focused – that's all.' She'd spent quite a few sessions training with Anya, and despite her slightly cold, practical manner, Jessie was starting to like her. Apart from the relentless training she seemed to expect from her partner. *Twenty hours!*

'Does she know you have other commitments?' asked Abby, helping herself to a second slice of pizza.

'What, GCV, you mean?' asked Jessie.

Abby nodded, widening her eyes as if to say, 'Obviously!'

'Yeah, I've mentioned it to her. She's not a big YouTube person though, so I dunno if she really gets it.'

'Ooh! Speaking of not getting it, you'll never guess who wants to make their first ever YouTube appearance guesting with Prankingstein?' said Abby. She looked around the whole restaurant as if about to confide a huge state secret, rather than news about her prankster brother and his friend's channel. 'Seriously, you guys are going to love this!'

Hermione twiddled her straw. 'I saw they did a shout-out recently asking for volunteers for their next challenge. Is it Eric?'

'Nope. A girl!' said Abby jubilantly.

'Do we all know her?' asked Hermione.

'Unfortunately for us, yes.' Abby pulled a sour face.

The penny dropped as Jessie realized who she meant. She screamed, causing the family at the neighbouring table to look over in surprise, including the toddler who knocked a plate of garlic bread off his high chair in excitement.

'Sorry,' Jessie mouthed at his mother. 'Surely not?' she said, looking to Abby for confirmation.

Abby nodded triumphantly.

'Who?' said Lucy and Hermione in unison.

'Shall we give them a clue?' said Abby.

'Sure!' Jessie thought for a moment, then put on a high-pitched screechy voice. 'Oh hi, have I mentioned your channel is ridiculous? Why don't you just drop dead, you have like *no* talent. As we saw with Abby and Lucy's TERRIBLE performance in *Grease*, which was MY chance to shine, not theirs. Ooh, it's a boy – quick, pass me some lipgloss!'

The diners at the next table stared again as Jessie took her voice an octave higher and gestured enthusiastically. 'Anyway, I've never made any videos in my life, but I love leaving mean, negative comments on your channel! Just because that's the kind of jealous, untalented person that I am. Ooh, there's another boy – time to restyle my hair again!' Jessie flicked her entire head of hair to the other side, getting some of it into her pizza. Her friends roared with laughter. 'I assume that's who you mean, Abs,' she added in her regular voice. 'Sorry,' she mouthed again to the neighbouring table.

'You got it!' said Abby.

'Ergh – what does *Dakota* of all people want with Prankingstein?' asked Hermione.

'That's what I'm trying to work out,' said Abby. 'Josh said she was very insistent in her messages when she emailed them. Said she'd go along with whatever they had planned for the video. They know she's a massive pain, but they thought she might be funny.'

'There's no stopping that g-girl.' Lucy sighed.

Jessie drummed her fingers on the table. 'It makes no sense,' she said, wracking her brain. 'Dakota likes fashion, expensive hair products and – er – being a complete snob. Why would she want to appear on a channel that's all about having fun and messy pranks? Surely she thinks she's above that? Unless –' She stopped herself, glancing over at Abby.

'Unless what?' demanded Abby, although Jessie had a feeling she knew exactly what she was about to say.

'Unless . . . she's got her eye on Josh or Charlie?'

'Yeah – n-now that she and Ben are over, m-maybe she wants to get her claws into a new guy,' said Lucy. 'She's been k-kinda flirty with Charlie in the past, h-hasn't she?'

'No,' said Abby abruptly.

Jessie exchanged glances with Lucy and Hermione. Abby had a weird on-off thing with Charlie, although they'd never actually admitted to being an item.

'Maybe it's Josh she likes – ew!' Abby grimaced. 'He'd never have time for her. I feel sorry for her really!'

Despite her casual words, Jessie noticed Abby pushing her pizza around her plate miserably.

'Well, let's wait and see if this video actually happens,' Jessie added cheerfully. 'I'm sure the mystery will be revealed soon. I for one cannot wait to find out what's going on.' Jessie loved the Prankingstein boys and their insane videos. 'It's going to be funny, that's for sure. Prankingstein and Dakota – jeez, it's just so wrong!'

Hermione's phone beeped and she took it out of her bag. 'Oh no.' She put it down again and sighed. 'My dad is driving me crazy.'

'Why?' asked Lucy sympathetically. 'Amy s-stuff?'

Hermione nodded, and there was a brief silence.

Jessie didn't know what to say, so she flagged down the waitress and ordered a chocolate milkshake. They all knew about Hermione's parents' divorce, and her dad's relationship with a woman from work, but Jessie always felt a bit awkward when the topic came up. Lucy was closer to Hermione, and Abby had divorced parents so could relate to some of what she was going through, but Jessie never knew what to say.

'Sorry to ruin the mood, guys,' said Hermione. 'It's not that bad – it's just that Dad keeps hassling me to go out for a meal with him, Amy and Felicity.' She shook her head in disbelief. 'Sure, Dad – I'd love to get to know the woman you cheated on Mum with, and her oh-so-charming daughter who trolled our channel!'

'Jeez!' said Jessie, her awkwardness forgotten as she remembered Felicity's horrible comments on their videos. 'Why would you *ever* want to hang out with *her*? Your dad must realize that's never going to happen!'

'You would think!' agreed Hermione. 'He keeps saying that Felicity only made the comments out of hurt, because her parents were divorcing too, and she's only eleven, so I should forgive her.' She rolled her eyes. 'Not happening. Anyway, let's change the subject.' She took a notebook out of her bag. 'Do we want to go through the outstanding GCV business while we're all together?'

'YES!' cried Abby.

Jessie yawned. While she loved making videos with the girls, she sometimes thought the others got a bit carried away with all the agendas and note-taking. Still, it was fun to watch Abby doing her thing, and she sat back and slurped contentedly on her milkshake as their chairperson sat up, pushed back her hair energetically and started to go through the agenda.

'First things first. SummerTube! Only twelve weeks and counting until our first convention, and our first ever panel. Hermione – jot down as follows. We need to fine-tune our outfits, make sure that our videos are slicker and more entertaining than ever. Have you seen SassySays's latest videos? We should look to her for inspiration. She's got so much creativity and energy – plus she's hilarious. Obviously we are too, but you know what they say, always room for improvement! OK, next. We need to keep an eye on our subscriber count, line up some potential collab partners . . .'

VLOG 3

Prankingstein: 100 Chicken Nugget Challenge 6:48

FADE IN: ABBY'S KITCHEN.

JOSH and CHARLIE are sitting at the kitchen table with a pile of fast-food boxes in front of them.

JOSH

Hi, PrankingFans! How's everybody doing? So today, as previously announced, we are doing the Chicken Nugget

Challenge, where we have to eat one hundred

nuggets in ten minutes!

CHARLIE

And luckily we have a surprise guest to help us.

(makes a wry face)

Dakota.

DAKOTA, in a tight red dress, pops up between them and

waves wildly.

DAKOTA

Hey guys! Sooo thrilled to be here and thanks for inviting me.

I'm so glad I could make it!

CHARLIE

You volunteered. Like, five times.

JOSH

Anyway, on with the challenge! So we've got one hundred

chicken nuggets in front of us here,

along with a load of sauces . . .

which we need to eat in ten minutes.

Ready?

CHARLIE

Oh, yeah . . . Smells so good! I've

been saving myself for this.

DAKOTA

I just lurve chicken nuggets with barbecue sauce. Squee!

CHARLIE

(making a face)

Squee? Squee?!

JOSH

Shut up! I'm starting the timer . . . NOW! And we're off!

DAKOTA begins delicately eating the nuggets.

DAKOTA

Watch me. Here I go . . . One . . . two . . . three . . .

CHARLIE

OK, Dakota, that's great – but you don't have to count out loud!

JOSH

I've had four already! This is going to be so easy.

MONTAGE: Sped-up footage of them all eating nuggets. Timer is now down to five minutes. Empty nugget boxes scattered around.

CHARLIE

We seem to be slowing down . . . and there's still lots of nuggets left . . .

DAKOTA

Here, have some of this, Charlie!

DAKOTA feeds him a nugget dipped in sauce.

DAKOTA (CONTINUED)

Sweet and sour . . . just like you!

JOSH

Ha ha! Should I leave you two alone?

CHARLIE

(crossly)

Don't be ridiculous! Just keep eating.

DAKOTA pats her stomach.

DAKOTA

I don't know how many more I can eat . . . I've got quite a

small appetite, which is why I'm so slim!

DAKOTA smirks.

JOSH rolls his eyes.

DAKOTA (CONTINUED)

But I'm not a quitter!

MONTAGE: More fast-forwarded eating.

DAKOTA burps loudly. She looks pale.

DAKOTA

Ooh! Sorry about that . . . but

I'm feeling a bit . . . er, where

is your bathroom?

DAKOTA rushes out of view.

CHARLIE

(mouth full)

Josh, you might need to go and check on her.

JOSH

Whaaat? Why me?

CHARLIE

Because it's your house and you might have to clean it up!

JOSH

OK . . . but stop the timer. I don't want to lose the challenge

because of her . . . and we were doing so well!

CUT TO: LATER.

CHARLIE

OK, one down, but the Prankingstein

boys are back! Thirty nuggets and three

minutes to go . . . Let's kill this!

JOSH

Kinda lost my appetite a bit . . . I'm

getting some water . . .

CHARLIE

No, that's just a waste of time. C'mon Josh!

DAKOTA appears, stroking her hair.

DAKOTA

I'm back too! Soooo sorry I let you down, guys, but I guess I'm

just a bit too delicate for this . . .

(giggles)

Can I help?

DAKOTA goes to wipe CHARLIE'S brow with a napkin.

CHARLIE

Ugh, get off me! There's only one minute to go, and still twelve

nuggets left! Josh!

JOSH

I'm going to burst.

JOSH burps loudly a few times.

JOSH (CONTINUED)

OK, go go go!

JOSH continues stuffing nuggets into mouth without chewing.

DAKOTA

Ten . . . nine . . . eight . . .

CHARLIE

So close!

CHARLIE rams multiple nuggets into his mouth at once.

DAKOTA

Three, two, one!

Timer goes off. CHARLIE turns
over last box. It is empty!

DAKOTA (CONTINUED)

Yay! You did it! You're both amazing!

CHARLIE

Whatevs . . . I just know I never want to see

another nugget again!

JOSH

OK, so we managed to eat one hundred nuggets in ten

minutes! Thanks for watching! Let us know if you enjoyed the

challenge with a thumbs-up and, as always, send us your

requests for your future challenges!

DAKOTA

(pouting)

Byeee!

FADE OUT.

Views: 4,000

Prankingstein subscribers: 5,400

Comments:

***jazzyjessie*:** Hahaha! Puke-ota strikes again

StalkerGurl: Josh still looks cute even with his mouth full of nuggets! xox

peter_pranks: Easy . . . I could have smashed 100 by myself.

queen_dakota: My YouTube debut ♥

prankingstein_fan_1: Hamburger challenge next, please!

(scroll down to see 22 more comments)

Chapter
Four

8:08

Jessie: That's put me off chicken nuggets for life, ha ha!

8:10

Abby: Hahaha! So wrong. Josh says Charlie couldn't wait to get rid of her. When they stopped filming, she kept trying to hang around, but Charlie said he had somewhere to be and just left her with Josh.

8:12

Jessie: Your poor brother!

8:13

Abby: I know . . . she didn't stick around for long though. I almost feel a bit sorry for her.

8:13

Jessie: So you think she likes Charlie??

8:14

Abby: Hashtag obviously!! Just cos I do.

8:14

Jessie: You do, hey?? ;)

8:17

Abby: Well I mean he's a nice guy ha ha. 😊 ANYWAY. Ready for our video later?

8:18

Jessie: I'm kinda nervous ha! But can't wait! See you later xx

Jessie hopped off the bus in front of the sports centre, putting her phone away. She was looking forward to doing some beam work today – she always tried to practise on walls and the edges of pavements when she was outside, but there was nothing like using the proper equipment to really challenge yourself. She knew that a couple of the other girls had their own beams at home, but she didn't want to ask her parents when money was already a bit tight. Besides, there was nowhere for a beam to go. It would reach across the whole sitting room, and Jake and Leon would be furious if it blocked the TV.

'Hi, Jessie!' said Anya, getting out of a car. She waved to the petite blonde woman at the wheel before she drove off.

'Hi! Was that your mum?' asked Jessie.

Anya nodded. 'She used to be a gymnast, you know.'

'No way! Like, a professional?' Jessie couldn't believe Anya hadn't mentioned this before. No wonder she had such a serious attitude towards her training.

'Yes – she was ranked quite highly for a couple of years,' said Anya proudly as they walked in together.

They reached the changing rooms and said hi to a few of the other girls from their class.

Anya lowered her voice. 'I don't want everyone knowing. I'll tell you about her later.'

'Oh, OK – no problem!' said Jessie in surprise. If her mum had been a professional gymnast, she would shout it from the rooftops. She started changing, wondering if Anya had a beam and other equipment at home, or old photos or videos of her mum competing. Then she was distracted by Emily, another girl in her group, asking her about Dakota's weird appearance on Prankingstein.

'OK, gang – so half an hour of individual beam and floor work, and then into your pairs,' said Laila after the warm-up. She stopped by Jessie. 'Any decisions made yet, Miss I'll Have a Think About It?'

Jessie noticed Anya looking over curiously as she overheard the question. 'Kind of,' she replied, desperately stalling for time. 'Can we talk about it at the end of class?'

Laila smiled patiently. 'OK, but we only have a week to sort out the entry forms, which your parents will need to sign, so let's make a decision today.'

Jessie exhaled loudly, and Laila tugged her ponytail.

'No need for sighs! It doesn't matter if you don't feel ready this time; we'll have plenty of other opportunities to work towards.'

'What about Anya though?' asked Jessie anxiously. 'If I don't enter, I mean?'

'I don't think anyone else is quite ready to be her partner at this level,' said the coach carefully. 'It's a tough competition. But you have to do what's best for you.'

That means she won't enter Anya without me, Jessie thought. Out of the corner of her eye she saw her partner's shoulders droop slightly. *What do I do now??* She joined the queue for the beam. On the one hand she was excited at the chance to enter her first serious competition, but on the other she worried she didn't have time to prepare for it well, and she didn't want to embarrass herself and Anya. The Easter holidays were coming to an end, and with them, all that extra training time. And with SummerTube round the corner, how could she commit to preparing for both?

Her worries were soon forgotten as she stepped up and performed a neat tuck somersault on the beam. A couple of girls who had been watching cheered. 'Thank you, thank you,' she said, taking a bow. That was the first time she'd landed perfectly on the first go, without wobbling, and a rush of happiness swept over her. *If only someone had been filming me!*

But her luck didn't last. As she and Anya worked on their pairs routine in the second half of the class, she sensed that her partner was going easier on her than normal.

'Argh!' she cried as she messed up an aerial cartwheel for the third time (the kind where your hands aren't allowed to touch the ground). 'I'll get it soon, I promise.'

Anya shrugged. 'Don't worry. It took me a long time to learn this too.'

'OK, thanks. I can visualize it in my mind, but when I try to do it for real, it just turns into a giant fail!' said Jessie. 'And the more I think about it, the more I mess it up!' She cleared her throat nervously. 'It's this kind of thing that makes me think maybe I'm not quite ready, you know . . . for the competition?' She glanced at her partner.

Anya didn't respond. Then after a pause, she said, 'You want a drink? I've got some coins.'

They stepped out into the hallway through the double doors, and Anya selected a bright blue energy drink from the machine for them to share. As Jessie took a massive gulp, Anya talked quickly.

'When I first met you, I also thought you weren't ready. And even though I wanted to be in the competition, I didn't want to enter if I thought we were going to make fools of ourselves. You were VERY unpolished.' She stared at Jessie critically.

Jessie spluttered and lowered the drink. 'I wasn't *that* bad! And it was only a few weeks ago!'

Anya calmly took the bottle from her. 'Anyway, I'm trying to tell you you've improved very much. I'm really impressed, and I think we can do this competition. Once we've figured out our routine, it's just a case of practice, practice, practice.' She whacked the bottle against her hand three times to emphasize her point.

'That's the thing,' said Jessie awkwardly. She eyed the other girls through the glass pane in the door and briefly wished that she were paired with one of them instead. 'Even though I am SO committed to gym, I have other interests too, and I don't know if I have—'

'YouTube, you mean?' interrupted Anya.

'Yep, that's one of them!' said Jessie. 'I can definitely do both – in fact my friend Abby is doing a video with me later for our channel, which is how to do make-up for a gymnastics competition.'

'What does she know about it?' asked Anya suspiciously. 'Is she a gymnast too?'

'No!' Jessie laughed trying to imagine Abby on a beam. 'But she loves make-up more than anyone I know, and she's done all this research online.'

Anya sniffed.

'Anyway,' continued Jessie, 'the point is, making videos takes a really long time, more than most people realize, and that's on top of schoolwork and other stuff at home. I just don't know if I can drop everything to focus on our training.' She noticed Laila looking at them questioningly through the double doors. 'But then again, who knows when another competition will come along . . .' She tailed off uncertainly.

'Look,' said Anya firmly. 'It's only a few weeks away, so if we go for it now, yes you'll have to train hard for a while, but after that you can decide to stop and never enter a competition again.' She smiled at Jessie. 'I know you can do this – you just need to believe in yourself!'

Jessie pondered. 'I suppose – and it's not like my friends don't have other activities as well.' She thought of Hermione and her books, Abby and drama (and Abby and boys), and Lucy volunteering at the city farm. Then she remembered how good she'd felt up there on the beam, pretending to be a star. When she executed a move perfectly, it was an even bigger rush than vlogging! She stared at Anya's pale, hopeful face. 'OK – here's the deal. We can enter, and I'll do my absolute best—'

Anya squeaked and punched the air.

'IF,' continued Jessie, putting her hand out, 'you promise not to hate me if we don't win gold.'

Anya nodded fervently.

'AND,' Jessie added, 'if you let me meet your mum and steal all her pro tips!'

Jessie got home and found her dad, Leon and Jake watching a *Star Wars* film in the sitting room. 'Where's Maxy?' she asked, helping herself to a handful of Doritos.

'Gabriella took him out for a walk to the park,' said her dad, patting the sofa. 'Come and join us?'

'In a minute. Is there any lunch around?' Jessie's

appetite was always bottomless after gym.

'Leftover sandwiches in the kitchen,' said her dad. 'I tried a couple of new fillings: one with—'

'Ssssh,' said Leon and Jake in unison.

'This is an important bit,' added Jake, turning up the volume.

'So? You must know every line of this by now,' said Jessie with a grin. She raised an eyebrow. 'How many times have you seen this one?'

'Five,' said Leon.

'Seven,' said Jake.

'Honestly, how are you not bored out of your skulls?!' She wedged herself between them on the sofa, to much moaning. 'Anyway, Dad, I have a thing for you to sign for gym.' She rummaged in her bag and excitedly handed him the form.

'What's this in aid of?' asked her father.

She couldn't wait to tell him, now that she'd made up her mind. 'Well, Laila thinks Anya and I are good enough to enter an under-fifteens pairs competition that's coming up,' she said proudly. 'It's an inter-club thing. I've been wondering about entering something like this for ages, and now I've got time to prepare for it properly.' She grinned. 'We're the only ones entering from the whole group!'

'Can you have this discussion somewhere else?' said Leon, pointing to the TV.

'Yeah, nobody cares,' said Jake, though he glanced over at Jessie, and she could tell that he was secretly quite impressed.

'Boys! The Emperor can wait for one second,' said her father. 'This is great news, Jess – can we come and watch you on the big day?'

Jessie froze – she hadn't thought that far ahead. None of her family had seen her perform a whole routine in ages, though she had asked her parents to come and witness her backwards walkover when she first managed it in the garden.

'I don't know,' she told her dad. 'But the venue's pretty big, so I bet you're allowed loads of guests! I'll find out.'

'What's the date? I'll put it straight on the kitchen calendar!' said her dad.

'It's on the form,' said Jessie, pointing.

She looked again. For some reason, the date rang a bell, but she shrugged it off.

'I'm busy that day,' said Leon. 'Washing my hair.'

'SHUT UP,' said Jessie, then felt annoyed with herself for allowing him to wind her up. She glanced at his buzzcut. 'You barely have any hair to wash. Anyway – whatever! I don't even want you there. It's no big deal.'

'I've got plans too,' said Jake, deadpan, as ever trying to be as cool as his big brother.

Despite their teasing, she knew they were proud of her, and as she walked into the kitchen she felt a little shiver of excitement at the thought of performing in front of them and Mum. Now she had to tell the girls!

VLOG 4

9:22

FADE IN: ABBY'S BEDROOM.

ABBY and JESSIE are sitting at the dressing table. Lots of make-up lying about. They both wave to the camera.

> ### ABBY AND JESSIE
> Hi, guys!

ABBY

So today I'm going to do Jessie's make-up. I can't wait –
I've been dying to get my hands on her for years, and
now she's entering her first serious competition,
so what better time?

JESSIE

As you know, I don't usually wear much make-up, but now that
I'm going into more competitive gymnastics, I need to think
about my look. Apparently, eye contact with the judges is really
important – along with smiling . . .

(she grins)

So defined eyes are a must!

JESSIE looks around at all the make-up.

JESSIE (CONTINUED)

Not sure I need this much though, Abs!

ABBY

Don't worry – let's get started. First of all you need to
moisturize all over . . .

JESSIE applies and blends in moisturizer all over her face.

ABBY (CONTINUED)

Good! You've got great skin, so I don't think you need any
foundation, and anyway we wouldn't want it all to melt off if
you sweat during a competition!

JESSIE

Ew! Yuck! No foundation, please.

ABBY

BUT I do think you could use a bit of blusher on the apples of
your cheeks, just a hint. This is quite a bright red, which should
suit your skin tone.

ABBY brushes blusher on to JESSIE's cheeks.

ABBY (CONTINUED)

How's that?

JESSIE

Yeah, good.

JESSIE gives a thumbs-up.

ABBY

OK – now for the eyes. I'm going to curl your lashes first before

we apply any make-up. If you wanted a more dramatic look,

you could even put on false eyelashes . . . But let's leave that

for another day. Hold still!

ABBY moves to curl JESSIE's eyelashes. JESSIE looks freaked out.

JESSIE

What even is that? It's like a medieval instrument of torture . . .
but really tickly!

ABBY

Trust me, it works! OK, so now I'm applying some sparkly white
eyeshadow to your lids, to help
them shimmer. Next up, some
colour . . . What colour is your
competition leotard?

JESSIE

Turquoise – my favourite!

ABBY

Awesome – I have turquoise . . .
so let's put some on the eyelids.

ABBY starts applying with brush.

ABBY (CONTINUED)

And then use some black eyeliner both top and bottom to
make your eyes really stand out. Stop jiggling, Jessie – you've
got to hold still!

JESSIE

I'll try.

ABBY applies eyeliner.

ABBY

OK. Not bad . . . What do you think?

JESSIE looks at herself in the mirror.

JESSIE

Wow!

ABBY

Not finished yet! So let me brush
on the mascara – both top and
bottom – there we go! I think that
looks great! Nobody can help noticing
your gorgeous big eyes now. Last but
not least, some lipgloss. Ta-da!

JESSIE

Amazing! No way those judges will miss me now! Thanks, Abs!

ABBY

And what about your hair – will you put it up? If so, you'll need
a scrunchie . . .

JESSIE

Yeah, I have one – it matches my competition leotard. I think
my coach would prefer my hair up.

ABBY uses a scrunchie to secure JESSIE's hair in a tight bun.

ABBY

OK, let's go downstairs and show the boys!

CUT TO: ABBY'S FAMILY ROOM.

JOSH and CHARLIE are on the sofa playing computer games.

ABBY (CONTINUED)

(filming them)

Have you seen how gorgeous Jessie looks in her competition

make-up?

CHARLIE

Wow! You look like a pro. So how about a gymnastics display

then? Can you do the splits?

JESSIE

Can I do the splits???

JESSIE proceeds to do front split and middle split in rapid succession.

JESSIE (CONTINUED)

Does that answer your question? How about you!

CHARLIE

Impossible . . . I think I'd literally split in two!

ABBY

Go on, have a go, guys – you've got the master here to teach you. Get up off that sofa, you pair of lazybones!

Rapid shots of CHARLIE and JOSH trying and failing to do splits and ending up collapsed on the floor in weird positions.

JESSIE

Oh dear! I know it's a bit harder for guys, but still . . . that was tough to watch!

CHARLIE

So hard! I didn't realize . . .

JOSH

I didn't realize how much it would hurt . . . argh!

JESSIE and ABBY laugh.

ABBY

At least sometimes you admit girls are better than boys!

JESSIE

That's all for today. If you enjoyed this video give us a thumbs-up down below! Byee!

FADE OUT.

Views: 5,333

Subscribers: 11,342

Comments:

MagicMorgan: Stunning, girl!

GabsDoesGym: *Awards you a perfect 10 for make-up.*

lucylocket: Lol at the guys doing the splits.

Amazing_Abby_xxx: I know! Hahaha.

ShyGirl1: Good luck in the competition, Jessie!

leotard_babe: Amazing! Now you need a matching manicure

(scroll down for 20 more comments)

Chapter Five

'I can't believe the holidays are over already,' moaned Jessie as they filed into assembly on the first day back. 'And is it because I haven't seen them in a while, or are Dakota and her minions looking extra smug today?'

In the row ahead, Dakota, Ameeka and Kayleigh were chatting animatedly, looking around with excited, slightly nervous grins on their faces, Dakota flicking her hair back and forth even faster than usual.

Hermione groaned. 'You're right. There's definitely something up with them. Even Ameeka is smiling, which is a rare event.' She lowered her voice as Mr McClafferty the headmaster arrived onstage. 'Watch yourself, ladies.'

Jessie shuddered as she exchanged anxious glances with the others. Lucy in particular looked tense, and Jessie remembered the time Dakota had set her up in assembly, which ended with a painfully embarrassing telling-off by the headmaster in front of the whole school.

'Well, girls and boys, welcome back to the summer term,' began Mr McClafferty, placing a messy folder of papers on the podium. 'I hope you've had a refreshing and restorative break and are feeling re-energized and ready to work.'

Jessie smothered a giggle as Abby rolled her eyes to the ceiling.

'Now –' he consulted the first piece of paper – 'I'm going to get several announcements out of the way before spending a little time reflecting with you all on the theme of perseverance. Which seems apt for exam season.'

Jessie sighed. This was going to take a while. *So why was Dakota sitting up so attentively?* she wondered suspiciously. Mr McClafferty's beginning- and end-of-term 'reflections' could drift on for hours and they could send even the most well-meaning student into Snoresville. Jessie had even seen their teacher Miss Piercy close her eyes once during a particularly lengthy assembly.

'Announcement number one,' began Mr McClafferty. 'We are taking a zero-tolerance approach to chewing gum this term. You will be made to spit it out in class, and if caught more than once you will get a detention.'

Fine, thought Jessie. *As long as you don't apply it to chocolate too.*

'OK, second announcement. The summer prom. In previous years, this event has been a special privilege for Years Ten and above. But Year Nine, I have good news for you – the prom will now be open as well to those of you who want to come.'

There was a brief pause, as the assembly hall of students digested this unexpected news. Then the Year

Nines broke out in cheers, while the kids from the older years looked annoyed by the announcement.

'Amazing!' whispered Jessie, surreptitiously taking a packet of gummy worms out of her skirt pocket in celebration and offering them around. 'But I don't get it – why have they changed the rules?'

'Who cares? It's the best news ever!' responded Abby. 'Finally, a forward-thinking move by this stupid school. Dress shopping, here we come!'

Jessie looked ahead and saw Dakota high-five her friends. Then, unbelievably, Dakota stood up, tossed her hair back, and walked calmly to the side of the stage at the front of the room.

'Er, guys. What is Dakota doing?' Jessie said through a mouthful of gummy worm.

'And how has her school skirt got even shorter since the beginning of assembly?' added Hermione wonderingly.

To Jessie's surprise, Mr McClafferty welcomed Dakota on to the stage. 'Dakota, one of our most promising and community-minded Year Nine students, will explain to you a bit more about how the idea came about.' He paused as Kayleigh and Ameeka whooped and hollered loudly from the audience. 'OK, off you go, Dakota.'

'Thanks, Mr McClafferty!' trilled Dakota, joining him by the podium. 'So, yeah, over Easter I was talking to my parents about, like, equal rights for our age group, and how in some US states you can go to prom earlier, at thirteen. My dad realized it was a clever and well thought out argument and decided to talk to Mr McClafferty about it.' She grinned. 'They've been in contact already about my dad's fundraising contributions for a new science lab. Anyway, it's all worked out so well, and – without sounding vain – I'm proud of what I've achieved for us all. Well, most of us – sorry, Years Seven and Eight! Everyone else: see you at prom!'

Jessie could hardly believe her ears. 'So, Dakota's dad bribed the school,' she summarized flatly. 'That's why the rules have changed.'

'Unbelievable,' said Eric behind her. 'Does she really want to go to prom that much?'

'And do we really need a new science lab?' groaned Abby.

Now that they knew Dakota was behind it, everyone's prom excitement was fading fast.

Nervously eating another worm, Jessie watched as Dakota proudly took her seat. *What on earth is she up to?* she wondered. She couldn't help but suspect that this was part of a bigger plan.

Onstage, Mr McClafferty shuffled some papers. 'Thank you, Dakota. So, Year Nines,' he said, 'you may add the date to your diary – 7th July. Another incentive to work extra hard this term. Now on to my thought of the day.' He stepped out to the side of the podium, happily stretching his arms out in front of him as he relaxed into the sound of his own voice. 'You may have heard the saying, if at first you don't succeed . . .'

*

Seven hundred hours later – or so it seemed to Jessie, whose bum had fallen asleep – Mr McClafferty declared that assembly was over.

'Year Nines, if you could stay behind for a few minutes, please,' he added.

'Y-you have got to be k-kidding me,' groaned Lucy.

Jessie gave her a sympathetic look. 'I know! What now? I feel like I've been superglued into this chair my whole life,' she said, stretching her legs out. 'Agh – pins and needles. Assembly is so bad for my muscles!'

As the other students and the teachers filed out of the room, Dakota took to the stage once again, this time flanked by Kayleigh and Ameeka. Jessie sighed – *not again*! Dakota looked confidently out at her peers, waiting for silence.

'Quiet,' bellowed Kayleigh after a few seconds.

'Yes, miss!' giggled Abby. 'Honestly, who do they think they are?'

The students all settled down, mainly out of curiosity.

'Hi again, everybody,' said Dakota, doing a cutesy

wave. 'So, Mr McClafferty asked me to give you a bit more of an update about the whole prom situation, as this will be our first year going.'

'How difficult is it to go to a prom?' whispered Hermione.

Jessie laughed out loud, until she realized that Ameeka was glaring at her. She chewed the inside of her cheek to keep quiet.

'There will be a questions section later,' said Ameeka sourly, 'if you could save your comments until then. Dakota, please continue.'

'Thank you,' Dakota said primly. 'So, I wanted to let you all know that I have been made head of the Year Nine prom committee, with Kayleigh and Ameeka here as my assistants. In this role I'll be choosing the theme, the decor, the refreshments, and so on.' She ticked off each item on her French-manicured fingers.

'BORING!' yelled some of the boys.

She ignored them, and despite herself Jessie was briefly impressed by Dakota's professional attitude.

'Of course,' continued Dakota, 'your feedback will be important to me when I'm making these crucial decisions, and so I wanted to let you know that I've had the unique idea of setting up a YouTube channel for this purpose.'

'A what?' cried Abby, her eyes wide.

Dakota smiled serenely. 'Some of you may have seen my guest appearance on the popular channel Prankingstein over the Easter holidays, and because it seems I'm quite the natural –' Jessie raised her eyebrows at Abby – 'I decided to play to my strengths and set up my own channel to stay in touch with you all about the prom.'

Kayleigh and Ameeka nodded along, murmuring 'great idea' and 'total natural, yeah'.

'I'll be sharing my tips on how to get ready, pose for photos, that kind of thing,' Dakota added. 'I'll let you know the second it's live. OK, everyone, that's it! Have a great day!'

Jessie's jaw dropped open in delayed shock. She

looked at the others, wondering whether to laugh or cry. Dakota setting up her own channel? To talk about a *prom*?

'Well, good l-luck to her,' said Lucy at lunch, when they were all together again. 'It's pretty h-harmless, right?'

'I guess,' said Hermione. 'Maybe she'll stop giving us such a hard time when she tries vlogging for herself and sees how difficult it can be.'

Jessie was amazed by how calm the others were being. Ever since Dakota had got her sent home from the skiing trip, she'd lost any patience with the girl.

'Guys – she's awful! I can't believe you'd encourage her. Anyway, we should probably just boycott this stupid prom. Abby?' She knew Abby would have plenty to say on the matter. 'Er, Abby?' she said again, realizing that her friend was staring at something on the other side of the cafeteria.

When there was still no reply, she followed Abby's gaze. Charlie was sitting at a small table with a girl from his year instead of with his usual crowd. The girl was taking a sip from Charlie's fizzy drink and, as Jessie watched, he nudged the can upwards into her chin, causing her to spill it and then burst out laughing.

Jessie immediately understood Abby's forlorn look: in Charlie World, this behaviour was medium- to high-level flirting.

'Who's that?' Jessie asked, finally getting Abby's attention.

'Huh? Who?' said Abby. 'Oh, her? I think she's called Louise.'

 'Wow, she's pretty,' said Hermione. Jessie saw her face fall as she noticed Abby's expression. '. . . I mean, she has nice hair, that's all,' she added, flustered.

'She doesn't s-seem that special to me,' said Lucy loyally.

Abby looked around the table. 'Guys. Please. You don't need to worry. Yes, she's pretty, and yes, Charlie obviously likes her company – I've seen them together a couple of times, actually.' Jessie noticed how hard she was trying to keep her tone light. 'But that's cool – me and Charlie are nothing! Like, when was the last time I even mentioned him?'

This morning at registration, replied Jessie silently, *when you were going on about how funny he was in our makeover video . . . and then again at mid-morning break when you mentioned his new haircut and whether it was better floppy . . .*

Lucy and Hermione also looked unconvinced by Abby's 'not bothered' attitude, but they all knew better than to challenge her.

'So, Dakota's channel – who's subscribing?' said Jessie cheerfully.

'Never mind that amateur,' said Abby. She glanced at her phone, then her face lit up. 'And besides, I've got real news! OMG – Tiffany wants us to do a collab on her RedVelvet channel before we all appear together at the SummerTube panel.' She scrolled down the message, waving her free hand around in excitement.

'She's thinking maybe we can do something fun at the city farm.'

The girls squealed in unison.

'I would l-love that!' said Lucy. 'I'll check with Sam and my m-mum. It would be great for the f-farm. They got loads of extra volunteers last time RedVelvet put it in her v-vlog.'

'Awesome! And in the meantime, if anyone has an idea for the theme of the video, that would be great,' said Abby, looking around the table expectantly. 'We could make our own one at the same time for the GCV channel.'

'Definitely,' said Jessie, trying to sound as excited as the others. She had loads of gym prep to think about, but maybe she could come up with some ideas. She knew she hadn't been the most creative member of the group lately. And thinking about gym, something else suddenly occurred to her. 'Remind me of the SummerTube date again, Abs?' she asked.

Abby looked at her as if she'd forgotten the date of

Christmas, or her own birthday. 'First weekend in July. Our panel is at 2.00 p.m. on the Saturday.'

'Cool, that's what I thought,' said Jessie. A horrible sick feeling crept up inside her . . .

VLOG 5

FADE IN: SHOPPING MALL.

JESSIE filming ABBY, HERMIONE and LUCY as they enter the mall.

JESSIE

(from behind camera)

Say hi, guys!

All the girls wave.

JESSIE (CONTINUED)

So here we are at the
mall, which is one of
our favourite weekend
haunts. And today
we have a special
mission . . . which is to
look at prom dresses.

LUCY

Yes! It's s-so exciting that there is going to be a p-prom this
spring at our school. It's the f-first time our year has been
included.

JESSIE

(off-camera, singing)

I'm so excited, and I just can't hide it!

HERMIONE

Don't make fun of Luce! She's the only one of us with a real boyfriend, so it's not exactly surprising she's excited about the prom.

ABBY

Whatever, ladies – I just want to look flawless! Let's try Primark and H&M first, then Topshop . . .

FADE TO: STORE DRESS DEPARTMENT.

ABBY (CONTINUED)

So here are some cool dresses. I kinda fancy something strapless myself . . . like this red one.

JESSIE

Wow – that's gorgeous! What about you, Lucy?

LUCY

Nooo . . . I wouldn't feel c-comfortable in something strapless.

Anyway, I'm so flat, it m-might fall down!

They all giggle.

LUCY (CONTINUED)

I'd like something long, s-swishy and romantic . . .

ABBY

Maybe this baby-blue one? It matches your eyes!

HERMIONE

Lucy, it does look perfect for you.

LUCY

OK, I'll t-try it on. What about you, H-Hermione?

HERMIONE

(awkwardly)

I don't really do glamorous . . . I'm not sure where to start.

ABBY

H! I've found the right thing for you – this bright yellow slinky dress. It would look stunning with your dark hair!

HERMIONE strokes her hair nervously.

HERMIONE

Hmmm. I'm not sure . . . it's very . . . well . . . bright! Like a neon highlighter.

ABBY

Just try it and we'll look for something else too . . . how about this deep purple?

HERMIONE

OK, I'll give them a go.

HERMIONE turns and points at JESSIE.

HERMIONE (CONTINUED)

Now it's your turn!

JESSIE

Help! You know I'm not really into dresses and girly clothes . . .

I'm not even sure I'll go . . .

LUCY, ABBY AND HERMIONE

(shrieking)

What??!!

ABBY

You HAVE to go! We're all going. You can't wimp out . . .

JESSIE

Well, OK. Maybe I can be there to film it . . . so do I really

need a dress? I can't see anything that's right for me. All these

sparkles and flounces and stuff.

ABBY starts rifling through the dress racks.

ABBY

OOOH! I've found it! The perfect thing!

JESSIE

What?

ABBY

A two-piece . . . it's like a crop top with these wide-legged trousers, harem style. You'll look hashtag *incredible*.

JESSIE

Not bad! OK – let's try them on.

MONTAGE: Girls walk to the changing rooms, picking up tags from attendant, and go into a large cubicle.

JESSIE (CONTINUED)

(whispering)

OMG! SHHH! Guess who's next door?!

LUCY, ABBY and HERMIONE all mouth 'Who?'

DAKOTA

(off-camera)

Oh, maybe this is the one . . . It really suits my colouring, don't you think?

AMEEKA

(off-camera)

It's AMAZING! I mean . . . WOW! You look like a princess . . .

DAKOTA

Let me see it in the big mirror . . .

DAKOTA comes into view and shrieks when she sees JESSIE filming.

DAKOTA (CONTINUED)

STOP THAT IMMEDIATELY! What are you doing?

You're spying on me!

LUCY

N-no, it was an a-accident . . . A c-coincidence, I mean . . .

DAKOTA

As if! You're just pathetic little losers following me around.

ABBY

Following you?! Don't be ridiculous!

And anyway, you look like a pink

marshmallow in that dress.

AMEEKA

Hey, Dakota, let's go. Things are

beginning to smell a bit bad round here . . .

DAKOTA

Yeah, and we've got that other shop to go to . . . They have personal shopping there and will treat us like queens. I didn't really like this dress anyway . . .

DAKOTA and AMEEKA leave.

MONTAGE: Each girl posing in the outfit she's trying on.

FADE TO: COFFEE SHOP.

All girls seated with hot drinks and some carrier bags in tow.

JESSIE

Here we are . . . all shopped out after an eventful day!

HERMIONE

OMG. That was soo embarrassing with Dakota . . .

LUCY

I know . . .

ABBY

So funny! And shopping-wise we had some wins,

some fails . . .

JESSIE

Let us know in the comments down below which outfits you

liked best. And we'll show you what we *actually* bought in a

later video!

ALL

(all waving)

Byee!

FADE OUT.

Views: 4,540

Subscribers: 13,230

Comments:

xxrainbowxx: Can you do an accessories haul too?

queen_dakota: Pathetic stalkers! Sad . . .

evie_bakes: New to this channel, you guys are funny ♥

SassySays: Can't wait to see what you got!

girlscanvlogfan: Jess you looked so cool in that outfit X

billythekid: Boring! More pranks please.

PrankingsteinJosh: Can't believe you Year Nines are crashing our prom ;) @billythekid, come to our channel – pranks galore!

emokid299: Has anyone watched Dakota's prom vlogs yet??

Thierryfromfrance: Hermione on fleek in the yellow!

(scroll down to see 32 more comments)

Chapter Six

One morning a few weeks after prom-dress shopping, Jessie arrived at the park and headed for the playground, where Abby had suggested meeting up. It was a warm spring day, the first Saturday of half-term, and on the spur of the moment she joyfully performed five cartwheels on the grass.

'JESS!' hissed Abby from behind the trunk of a huge tree, startling the life out of her. She was wearing a new look: black from head to foot. 'Come over here.'

'What the – why are you hiding?!' called Jessie. A hopeful look crossed her face. 'Are we going to prank the others?'

'No!' Abby beckoned to her impatiently. 'Stop drawing attention to yourself and *come here*!'

Jessie rolled her eyes and jogged over to the tree, brushing the dirt from her palms. 'What's going on?' She grinned, taking in Abby's black jeans and turtleneck. 'And, er, who died?'

Abby shrugged. 'I sometimes prefer dark colours, that's all. It's hashtag *sleek*.' She peeped around the tree trunk, then checked the time on her phone. 'I hope the others get here soon.'

Jessie frowned in confusion. 'Why the rush . . . ? Isn't the plan just to hang out, enjoy the nice weather, maybe go for chips?'

Abby said nothing, a devious expression on her face.

'And why are we hiding? . . . Abs!' Jessie sighed as Abby continued to ignore her. She knew there had to be some method to her madness, but, honestly, what was going on?

'Look! There's Hermione and Lucy,' she said in relief

as she saw the girls approaching the swings, arm in arm.

'Bring them over here. Quickly,' instructed Abby.

'Er, yes, boss!' Jess stepped out from the tree and waved. 'Hi, guys!' They didn't see her so she walked right over to them. 'Hey!' She tapped Hermione on the shoulder. They turned and greeted her, and she was relieved to see that they at least seemed to be in a cheerful mood.

'Hi, Jess! So, chicken or egg – which do you think came first? As in *really* think about it,' said Hermione. 'We've been talking about it the whole way here. I'm team chicken; Lucy's team egg.'

Jessie giggled at the randomness of the question. She started to give it some thought, then noticed Abby gesticulating furiously at her from behind the tree. 'Much as I'd love to get into this important subject, guys, Abby REALLY wants us to join her.' She pointed at the tree, and the others squinted in the sunlight to see.

'W-what is she doing over there?' asked Lucy. 'And

why is she dressed l-like Simon Cowell?'

Jessie laughed. 'I have literally no idea. She's been acting shifty since I got here and she refuses to explain anything.'

'Hey, guys, isn't that Charlie – and that girl Louise?' said Hermione, sideways nodding at a couple wandering towards the ice-cream van.

'Yes!' cried Lucy. 'Are they . . . on a d-date?'

Jessie looked at the couple, who weren't holding hands but were doing a good impression of two people enjoying each other's company, and suddenly things began to fall into place. She turned and saw Abby, who, like an attentive meerkat, had swivelled her head in Charlie's direction too.

'Come on,' Jessie said to the others, and they all gathered under the tree.

'Hi, Abs!' said Hermione, as Lucy attempted to greet her with a hug. But Abby wasn't interested, her eyes still fixed on Charlie and Louise, who had now joined the queue for ice cream.

'Abs, did you know they were going to be here?' asked Jessie accusingly.

Hermione flinched.

'Well, someone had to ask! Or is this just a mad coincidence?' Knowing Abby, she doubted it was the latter.

Abby shrugged. 'Josh may have mentioned something when I asked why he wasn't filming with Charlie this morning. And I just thought – hey, why not see what they're up to.' She turned slightly pink. 'Not that I care, like, AT ALL – but, you know, Charlie's our friend, so I thought we should support him.'

'From behind a tree?' said Hermione.

Jessie stifled a giggle.

'Doesn't r-really look like he needs our support,' added Lucy, as Charlie handed Louise a 99 flake while taking a huge lick of it for himself. Louise laughed and made a big deal of grabbing his wallet from his back pocket to buy herself a second one.

Jessie cringed in sympathy as Abby turned a darker

shade of pink. Poor thing – she really did like Charlie, but she was too proud to admit it. 'Anyway, we've seen them now,' said Jessie. 'What shall we do next? I've got two blissfully free hours before gym practice!'

'Come on,' said Abby anxiously, not listening. 'They're leaving.' She stepped out from underneath the tree and ran behind another one, a few metres closer to the ice-cream van.

Jessie exchanged baffled glances with Lucy and Hermione. 'Are we stalking them?' she mouthed, half in delight, half in shock.

Thirty minutes and a bus ride into town later, she had her answer. They'd had to creep on to the bus and crouch behind a woman with lots of shopping bags to avoid being noticed by Charlie and Louise, and now as they followed them into the local cinema, Lucy tugged on Abby's arm.

'Abs? I think maybe . . . w-we should leave them to it n-now?'

'Aren't you guys up for the cinema?' asked Abby

casually, hiding by the pick-and-mix counter as Charlie and Louise got in the queue for tickets. 'I haven't been in ages.'

'I went last weekend and I'm kind of broke,' said Jessie. 'So I don't really have the cash to go again, sorry!' Staying for a film would also make her late for gym, but she didn't think Abby was in the right mood to hear about that. 'Plus it's such a nice day outside, why don't we go and catch some rays?' She wiggled her sunglasses up and down, watching as Charlie and Louise filed into screen two, which was showing the latest Pixar film.

Hermione nodded. 'Yeah – besides, we're not going to be able to see much in there. I mean, we've already proved that they're hanging out, what more is there to know?'

Abby started to argue back, then her face fell and she gazed down at the popcorn-strewn carpet. 'You're right,' she said slowly in a small voice. 'All of you. I don't know what came over me. I just . . . from the minute I heard that Charlie and Louise had plans today, I had this crazy need to know every single detail.' She looked up. 'Sorry for dragging you into this.'

Jessie's heart went out to her. Personally she'd never had this big a crush on anyone before, but she could see it was making Abby miserable. Even though Abby had never properly admitted to liking Charlie, there was always chemistry between them, and it was a surprise to all of them to see him dating another girl. It looked like 'Chabby' was over for the foreseeable future.

'Hey, I watched SassySays's latest video yesterday,' Jessie said brightly, trying to change the subject. 'It was amazing! She did the One Hundred Layers of Lipstick Challenge.'

Abby was newly obsessed with the pink-haired YouTuber, who was about their age, and Jessie found her really funny too. Sassy always spoke super-fast and didn't seem to care if she messed up.

'I w-watched it too!' said Lucy, taking Abby's arm and guiding her out of the foyer into the street. 'She's so funny. Maybe we c-could approach her about doing a collab some time?'

Abby nodded enthusiastically. 'Hashtag *let's do it*.' But her voice still sounded flat.

12:03

Jessie: Sorry had 2 dash after chips, hope A has cheered up??!

12:08

Lucy: Kinda, she just bought a new lipgloss x

12:09

Jessie: Definitely a good sign 😊. Gonna film 'What's in my gym bag' after practice today, hopefully with Anya.

12:11

Lucy: Abs said you were doing that – good luck! Hope it's not just smelly socks ha ha! xx

Jessie: 😖

That afternoon, Jessie and Anya had a practice area to themselves in the sports centre. Jessie jumped on the beam and started pacing up and down it. She wanted to try a move where they walked towards each other from either end, did a somersault at exactly the same time, and met in the middle.

But Anya was preoccupied, standing in the corner of the room and flicking through her diary. 'Listen – I've counted down the days, and we have five weeks until the first weekend of July,' she announced. 'I'd like us to have the routine finalized by the middle of June –' she pencilled something frantically – 'which means we have two full weeks to practise it until we know it better than our own faces!'

'And it's on the Saturday, right?' asked Jessie, picking up one foot and trying not to wobble. 'The competition, I mean.'

Anya nodded. 'Yes, in the afternoon. Maybe we can go out afterwards to celebrate,' she said, a little shyly. 'If it goes well, that is.'

'Sure, sure.' Jessie grinned, jumping lightly off the beam and trying to ignore the panicky thoughts gathering in her head. It was no good, she'd been avoiding the issue for weeks and had to do something about it: *the competition date clashed with SummerTube!* They'd entered the gymnastics competition – but RedVelvet had already signed up Girls can Vlog for the panel event, too. Worst timing ever!! Why did the two most amazing things in her life have to be on the same day, in completely different cities?

'Don't worry – we can do this!' said Anya, misreading her anxious expression. 'Now, let's start with some backflips. Then you can tell me about this strange YouTube video you want us to make later.'

VLOG 6

FADE IN: JESSIE'S BEDROOM.

JESSIE and ANYA are sitting on Jessie's bed.

JESSIE

Hey, guys! So today I'm going to film with

my new friend Anya . . .

JESSIE points at ANYA, who waves uncertainly.

JESSIE (CONTINUED)

. . . who I met at gymnastics. We've been training together for

our pairs routine, so we've got to know each other

quite well. Say hi, Anya!

ANYA

(shyly)

Hi!

JESSIE

Anya's an amazing gymnast and

really puts me to shame . . . but I'm

trying to get better and keep up!

ANYA

Like I told you, you have good potential, Jessie, but you need to

practise more . . .

JESSIE

(laughs)

You see? She's a tough cookie! So today we thought we'd do our own version of the 'What's in my bag?' tag and reveal what's in our gym bags. Anya's going to kick off with hers cos it's much tidier . . . let's go!

ANYA

(hesitantly)

So it's important to plan ahead and pack your bag properly so that you have everything you might need – otherwise you might get to the gym and discover you are missing something essential – like your leotard or sports bra, say – and you won't be able to train.

JESSIE

You have a really cool backpack, Anya, whereas I'm still using this rubbish old duffle bag.

ANYA shows off her purple backpack.

ANYA

Yeah, I got this for Christmas. I love it! It holds tons of stuff

and has separate pockets for dirty clothes and trainers

as well as for drinks, and a small one for my jewellery. It

helps me keep it tidy!

JESSIE

Unlike mine . . .

(smiles guiltily)

So what's in there?

ANYA

First of all, my clothes: a leotard and shorts if I'm going to

gymnastics, plus a good sports bra if I'm working out at the

gym. And of course clean socks and trainers too if we're

training on the machines. For gymnastics we tend to be

barefoot though.

JESSIE

(encouragingly)

Awesome. What else?

ANYA

Music. It really helps me to
concentrate and focus while I'm
on the running machine. So I
have these cool headphones –
which I also got for Christmas.

ANYA puts on a pair of large pink headphones.

ANYA (CONTINUED)

Wearing headphones also means people don't talk
to me so much!

JESSIE

Yeah, I like training with music too. Helps to energize and
inspire me to try harder!

ANYA

Hydration is important, so I have my favourite water bottle. I also have quite a few protein bars to eat after class or exercise to top up my energy levels.

JESSIE

Hmm. I usually eat a Mars Bar . . .

ANYA

(shocked)

Not good for you to have all that sugar! You should try these cereal bars – delicious! Or maybe some nuts.

JESSIE pulls a comical face at the camera.

JESSIE

If you say so! Anything else in there?

ANYA

Yes – I also have a bag of grips and wrist guards, which

the coach sometimes recommends for strengthening my wrists. And finally in this pocket I keep my toiletries: face and body wipes for after

exercise if I don't have time for a shower. Extra hair ties, scrunchies and pins to keep my hair neat. Hand sanitizer and lip balm. And most important of all – DEODORANT!

JESSIE

Wow, it's amazing how much you've got in there! It's like Mary Poppins's bag! I also have dry shampoo, which helps keep my braids clean from sweat. And also this little teddy . . .

JESSIE shows a miniature white teddy on a key chain.

JESSIE (CONTINUED)

. . . which my Dad gave me for good luck!

ANYA

(blushing)

I didn't mention it, but I have a good-luck charm too.

ANYA holds up a tiny toy troll.

ANYA (CONTINUED)

It used to be my mother's mascot when she was competing. It brought her success, so I hope it does for me too!

JESSIE

Cute! So that was fun! You've inspired me to tidy out my gym bag and get organized!

JESSIE takes out some old sweet wrappers from her bag.

JESSIE (CONTINUED)

Thanks for watching, guys – let me know if you enjoyed this vlog about gymnastics, and we'll do some more. Put your suggestions in the comments down below!

JESSIE AND ANYA

(both waving)

Byee!

FADE OUT.

Views: 5,021

Subscribers: 14,002

Comments:

GabsDoesGym: Nice kit! People forget we have to work out in the gym too . . .

Amazing_Abby_xxx: Those headphones are goals!

PrankingsteinJosh: Will any of it help me with the splits?!

jazzyjessie: Ha ha, maybe a nice scrunchie Josh? x

Jakethechamp: Ew, sis – you've had that bag forever, it must stink!

queen_dakota: Sweaty gym gear – gross.

girlscanvlogfan: I want a good-luck troll too!

(scroll down to see 32 more comments)

Chapter Seven

The following Saturday, Abby sent the girls a message saying that she couldn't host their regular meeting at her house, so Hermione volunteered to have them all over instead. Jessie loved Abby's place. It was so big and spacious, with well-stocked cupboards and endless snacks, and the cute, energetic company of Weenie. But there were often baked goods on offer at Hermione's, and she let Jessie in wearing a flour-coated apron: always a good sign.

Jessie breathed in a delicious aroma. 'Smells yum! Hope that's for us, whatever it is.'

'Sure is! My mum's out and we have the place to

ourselves,' said Hermione, leading Jessie into the kitchen, where a large plate of white- and milk-chocolate-chip cookies sat in the middle of the table.

'Wow! I've forgotten what it feels like to have a place all to yourself.' Jessie laughed as she helped herself to the biggest, gooiest cookie on the plate. 'Wait, I don't think I've ever known what that feels like! Honestly, it's so busy at my house, and even though Gabriella is really nice, I miss my room so badly.' She waved at Abby who was pouring milk into four glasses.

'Hey, Jess,' said Abby. 'I was just explaining why I couldn't host today. My brother and Charlie were filming in our kitchen and I wanted to be, like, a million miles away.'

Jessie smiled sympathetically. 'Fair enough. Maybe we should swap houses!' Jessie hoped this Louise thing wouldn't put a permanent end to Abby's friendship with Charlie. Still, at least Abby didn't seem to be in too terrible a mood today after last week. Jessie knew she had to tell everyone about the date clash with

SummerTube and her gym competition, and she was dreading sharing the news.

The doorbell rang five times in quick succession.

'OK, OK – we can hear you!' said Hermione. 'Lucy's a bit keen today!'

A few minutes later they discovered why.

'Tiffany's f-finally spoken to my mom about Springdale,' Lucy began. 'And we're going to be f-filming there a week on Thursday, you know we have an inset half day at school? The farm's going to close early for us.'

The girls jumped on each other in excitement. They'd only filmed with Tiffany, better known as RedVelvet, a couple of times, and the huge, nerve-wracking thrill of filming with such a famous YouTuber was amazing. Jessie still couldn't believe Tiffany had taken them under her wing in the first place – and she was still star-struck whenever she saw her.

'What time?' Jessie asked, checking her phone. 'I'm meant to be doing an hour's practice at lunch with Anya that day; we're supposed to have the routine finalized by then. But I should be done by two, and I can get to the farm soon after.' She looked around anxiously. *When did my life get so crazy?!*

'That's fine,' said Lucy. 'Filming's not until three, which is the earliest T-Tiffany can do. We need to get there early to get ready – and Jess, you'll just have to hurry.' She grinned. 'This is g-going to be the most fun ever.'

'A week on Thursday is soon though,' said Abby, her excitement rapidly changing to panic. 'We need to get ready. H, have you got your notebook?'

Hermione waved it in her face.

'Right,' said Abby seriously, tapping her fingers on the table. 'What's the main theme of the video, and what are we going to wear?'

'Guys, that's the b-best bit,' said Lucy. 'Tiffany wants us to model her new line of workout T-shirts that she's designed for an animal-rescue charity! There are f-four big cat designs, so she s-said we could model one each.'

The girls gasped.

'She's got s-some cute animal masks for us to wear

too,' Lucy continued. 'That's why sh-she wanted to film at the farm – it all fits together perfectly. Plus we're getting our h-hair and make-up done professionally!'

The girls fell silent, suddenly extremely nervous and hardly able to believe their luck.

Jessie cleared her throat. 'Speaking of RedVelvet, I have a slight issue with . . .' she began, then stopped. She couldn't bear to mention the date clash and ruin everyone's mood. 'I can't believe we're gonna be MODELS!' she shouted instead, flinging her arms around her friends.

Ten days later . . .

'Yes! I think we've got it!' said Anya, pausing the music on her iPhone.

Jessie grinned. 'Really?' she panted. 'I'm hashtag *exhausted*!'

This had been their most intense session yet, but she'd been rehearsing by herself all week, and it was so reassuring to know that they'd managed the routine once without any major errors.

'It was great, very smooth. I'll go and get Laila so she can watch it once all the way through and give us some notes,' said Anya. 'Especially with that double flip – that's the only thing worrying me. I think she'll have finished her beginners class by now.'

'OK,' said Jessie, glancing at the clock. 'It'll have to be quick though.'

She picked up her phone from the side of the hall to send Abby a message saying she'd be a few minutes late to the Springdale filming. She gasped. Thirty-three missed calls and twenty-seven WhatsApp messages! Had something awful happened?

14:30

Abby: On your way? X

14:35

Lucy: The outfits are awesome, hurry!! Xx

14:47

> **Hermione:** Come on slowcoach! 😊

14:55

> **Abby:** Pick up the phone!! We're all waiting and you need your hair done! x

15:05

> **Abby:** WHERE ARE YOU?????

'FLIPPING FUDGE BISCUITS!' cried Jessie, her stomach dropping through the floor. 'What the—! I thought I had some time left?' She checked the time and realized the awful truth, her jaw dropping open. It was 15:05, not 14:05! The clock in the gym was an hour behind. No wonder she was exhausted, they'd been going for nearly two hours!

Running past Anya and Laila in the corridor, she shouted 'Sorry – gotta go – explain later!' and grabbed her clothes from the changing-room bench, throwing the coat over her leotard and rushing out of the building to the bus stop.

15:19

Jessie: ON BUS – BE THERE ASAP 😵

Twenty minutes later, she dashed past the entrance gates of Springdale City Farm and saw a group of people with cameras, lights and tripods set up near the stables. As she drew closer, she saw Abby, Hermione and Lucy wearing the animal T-shirts, their hair styled amazingly with loads of volume, sitting on a bale of straw and looking at someone's laptop. Their animal masks were perched on top of their heads.

'OMG, guys, I am SO SORRY,' she said. 'You won't believe this, but the clock was wrong in the gym.'

Lucy and Hermione looked up in concern, but Abby didn't even glance at her.

'Anyway,' she continued breathlessly, trying not to collapse on the floor. 'I'm here now – where's my T-shirt?

I can change super quickly.' She looked around. 'Where's Tiffany?'

'She left,' said Abby flatly.

'She – what?'

'She had another commitment tonight, so she was in a rush. We had to do the filming without you.'

Jessie swallowed. 'You've already done it? But . . . I'm only, like, an hour late – can't I just . . . ?' She trailed off, realizing in horror that the damage was done.

'Sorry, J-Jess,' said Lucy. 'She was on a really t-tight schedule and she brought loads of people to help with the sh-shoot who had to go too. The rest of these guys are just p-packing up.'

Jessie looked around and saw that the equipment was being put away in boxes. She felt tears spring up in her eyes. 'But . . . but who wore the fourth T-shirt?'

Abby stood up and stared at her, hands on her hips and eyes blazing. 'Exactly, Jess! That was our problem, when Tiffany asked where you were. She wanted the four of us in the four different designs, as planned. In the end she wore the T-shirt herself, but she wasn't too happy about it – she was meant to be wearing this amazing dress.'

Jessie gulped. 'I'm sorry – that's awful.' She summoned some courage and tried to smile. 'I bet the video's going to be incredible, though. I can't wait to see it!'

Lucy nodded. 'It was really fun. I can't b-believe you missed it.'

'Come and have a look, if you're interested,' offered Hermione glumly. 'Here's some of the footage.'

As Jessie took a seat on the bale of hay, Abby turned towards her. 'Oh, having a nice sit-down, are we? After all the hard work you've put in today?' she said meanly.

'Abs! Give her a break,' said Hermione. 'It was an honest mistake.'

'I promise I'll make it up to you guys,' said Jessie guiltily. She felt terrible – she hated letting people down. But at the same time, she was starting to feel a bit annoyed with Abby's lack of understanding. Anyone could make a mistake, and it wasn't her fault the clock had stopped working.

Abby laughed coldly. 'Well, you'll have to make it up to Tiffany, too. She trusted us to promote her T-shirts, and do a professional job today. Now she's doubting whether we're the right people to go to SummerTube with her.'

'Come on, she didn't actually say that!' said Jessie, rolling her eyes. She noticed Hermione and Lucy looking uncomfortable. ' . . . Did she?'

'Kind of,' mumbled Hermione, eyes still glued to the screen. 'She said four was a better number than three.'

Lucy nodded. 'And she wanted reassurance that we would all stick to our commitment and sh-show up to the panel event next m-month.'

'Look, she'll understand it was an innocent mistake, once I explain,' said Jessie, trying not to panic. 'It's not like I couldn't be bothered to show up.'

'You didn't even answer your phone, or reply to any of our messages!' said Abby accusingly.

'It was on SILENT because I was practising,' said Jessie angrily, her voice hoarse. 'I'm sorry, OK? What else can I do?'

'C-come on, guys,' said Lucy soothingly, still trying to mask her own irritation, Jessie thought. 'The video was made, and yes T-Tiffany was a bit annoyed, but it's not the end of the world. It was a one-off.'

'How do we even know that,' scoffed Abby. 'It's obvious Jess and her new BFF Anya are obsessed with spending every single second of their day preparing for their stupid competition, so this kind of thing probably *is* going to happen again.' She sighed, throwing her animal mask to the floor. 'We'll never be ready for SummerTube at this rate.'

'OH YEAH?' exploded Jessie, standing up and facing her. 'Well I can't come to your precious SummerTube anyway. It's on the same day as my "stupid competition".' She saw the news hit Abby and almost enjoyed watching the shock cross her face. 'And I didn't know what to do about it. I've been going back and forth about which thing to choose, but seeing how rubbish you think I am as a member of Girls Can Vlog, I guess I'd better choose the competition. At least Anya isn't permanently disappointed in me.'

Saying it out loud helped her actually reach a decision, and it felt good. Her heart pounding with adrenaline, she walked briskly away from the group . . . before bursting into tears a few moments later.

VLOG 7

Girls Can Vlog/RedVelvet Collab: Behind the Scenes at the Fashion Shoot!!

6:55

FADE IN: SPRINGDALE CITY FARM.

ABBY, LUCY and HERMIONE in Springdale City Farm kitchen, the makeshift make-up and hairstyling area. Curling tongs, hairbrushes and make-up all spread out.

ABBY

Hi, everyone! Today we're at Springdale City Farm, where we're going to be doing a collab with our

HERMIONE

(interrupting)

And amazing mentor . . .

ABBY

. . . The one and only RedVelvet! Also known as Tiffany! She's going to be launching her new range of exercise gear.

LUCY

Which features four endangered b-big cats – snow leopards, tigers, black panthers and j-jaguars – and will be raising money for charity.

ABBY

(practically squealing now)

And – OMG – we are going to be modelling

some of the clothes! I'm sooo stoked!

HERMIONE

(seriously)

Well, it's for a very good cause.

ABBY

The official video will be on the RedVelvet channel – we'll link it below – while ours is a behind-the-scenes extra treat. So now it's time to get our hair and make-up done! Hashtag *amaze*!

FADE TO: Girls now made-up and in their outfits: T shirts, each with a different big-cat mask on and matching leggings. TIFFANY is there too.

TIFFANY

Wow! You guys look incredible! Hermione, you look AMAZING in that tiger top. And, Abs, that snow leopard really suits you. Lucy, so slinky in that black-panther gear!

LUCY

I'm n-never taking this off!

TIFFANY

So where's Jessie? Can't wait to see her in that jaguar print!

Hope she's not going to be late . . .

ABBY

She won't be. I was very clear with her about the time.

TIFFANY

Well, we still have some time before we need to start filming.

Lucy, can you show me some of the cute baby animals we're

going to feature when we do the farm walkabout?

LUCY

Sure. W-well, there's lots to
ch-choose from: lambs, kid
goats, piglets, bunnies and lots
of chicks and d-ducklings.

TIFFANY

I love them all! Do you have a favourite you
want me to feature?

LUCY

Well, I adore the k-kid goats – Snowdrop's b-babies. They are
so cheeky and naughty!

TIFFANY

Done! That'll be my first stop.

LUCY

(coughs nervously and speaking quietly)

Tiffany, those of us who work at city farm are so g-grateful for
all your support. It m-means a lot and has really helped raise
awareness of what we do.

LUCY hands TIFFANY a bouquet of
flowers she'd been hiding behind
her back.

TIFFANY

Aww! I'm so touched!

TIFFANY gives LUCY a hug.

CUT TO: SPRINGDALE CITY FARM KITCHEN.

LUCY and HERMIONE alone
in kitchen. LUCY admiring her
hair in mirror.

LUCY

Imagine if we could look like
this every day!

HERMIONE

We wouldn't be allowed to wear this make-up to school . . .

ABBY

So unfair!

ABBY looks at her phone.

ABBY (CONTINUED)

Where is Jessie? I've been texting and calling her, and she's not

picking up . . .

HERMIONE

Maybe her phone's dead? Anyway, I'm sure she'll come. She

knows how important this is . . .

TIFFANY and LUCY enter.

TIFFANY

Still no Jessie?

HERMIONE

(quietly)

No . . . Not yet anyway . . . We just can't reach her.

ABBY looks as if she's going to burst into tears.

ADDY

I am soooo sorry.

TIFFANY

Don't worry, guys! It's disappointing, but we're out of time, so
we'll just have to move on to Plan B.

FADE TO: LATER.

TIFFANY enters in big-cat gear.

TIFFANY

G-growl! Meet the new Jaguar!

She twirls around and pretends to prowl.

TIFFANY (CONTINUED)

So without any further delay, let's start shooting!

LUCY

(voiceover)

All's well that ends well!

ABBY

(voiceover)

We're so grateful to Tiffany for this fab collab. Don't forget to

check out the big-cat collection website, which is linked in the

description box – and the main video, of course, which we'll

link the second it's out. Bye!

FADE OUT.

Views: 23,402

Subscribers: 16,023

Comments:

MagicMorgan: Oh no, what happened to Jessie?

queen_dakota: How unprofessional that she didn't

show up! #awkward

RedVelvet: Wow, cute video! Thank you guys again for your help xxx

girlscanvlogfan: Smashed it.

animallover101: I'm asking for the snow-leopard one for my birthday.

SassySays: Modelling with RedVelvet?! #goals

RedVelvetSuperFan: You guys are so lucky!!!!!

PrankingsteinJosh: Look at those subs soar!

aoife54: Did Jessie EVER show up??

(scroll down to see 239 more comments)

Chapter Eight

The next morning, Jessie awoke in a grouchy mood after an odd, stressful dream about filming a gymnastics video at Springdale. She'd been cartwheeling over the petting-zoo animals and trying to avoid landing in manure. *Weird.*

She looked at her phone and sighed as she saw the latest messages in the Girls Can Vlog group chat.

7:34

> **Lucy:** Still don't see why you didn't edit that stuff out of the video, Abs?

7:38

> **Abby:** Was just keeping it real!!

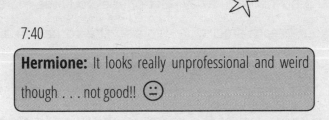

7:40

> **Hermione:** It looks really unprofessional and weird though . . . not good!! 😕

7:50

> **Abby:** Don't blame me! I'm not the one who was late!

Jessie felt sick. The others had been arguing about Abby's edit of the city farm video since last night, but she was staying out of it. She'd cringed when she'd seen the video because it made such a big deal of her no-show, and she agreed with Hermione and Abby that it looked unprofessional. Some of the comments were harsh too. She was pretty sure Abby had kept those bits in to upset her, out of spite. If so, it had worked – Jessie was dreading going into school and having to explain herself.

As Max hopped up on to her bed and tried to snuggle in with her over the covers, as he did most mornings, she pushed him away. 'Get off me, you little monster – your breath smells like Wotsits,' she complained. 'Why can't I ever get any privacy around here?'

His face fell and he stared at her disbelievingly before scurrying out of the room and erupting into wails of tears on the landing, screeching, 'I HATE JESS!'

Overcome with guilt, she jumped out of bed to scoop him up and cover him in kisses, but he wriggled out of her arms – still bawling – and ran off.

'Woah . . . what did you do to him?' asked Leon, emerging from his room down the hall. 'That screaming was loud, man.'

'Why don't you share a room with him and find out?' said Jessie, kicking some *Star Wars* toys out of the way before re-entering her room and slamming the door shut. She knew she was overreacting, but she didn't care.

At school she ignored her classmates' questions at

registration (*What happened? Are you quitting the* *channel?*), then half dozed through double history. She watched miserably as Abby, looking angry, passed a note to Hermione. Was it about her? She still hadn't talked to them since yesterday or sent any messages. At break she decided enough was enough.

'Hey, guys,' she said, joining them in the hall near the snack stall. She couldn't remember the last time she'd felt nervous around her friends. 'Look, I'm really sorry about yesterday. I was completely bummed to miss it.'

Hermione shrugged. 'Don't worry – we all get it wasn't your fault.'

'Totally,' agreed Lucy. 'It was a sh-shame, but it's all forgotten. Well, It w-would be, if the video had been edited properly.'

'Yeah, thanks for that, Abs,' said Jessie sarcastically, losing her cool despite her best efforts to stay calm. 'Really appreciate it.'

Abby rolled her eyes. 'It's nothing personal; I just

wanted to show the viewers that sometimes things don't go to plan.'

'Well, you've definitely accomplished that,' replied Jessie, 'and now everyone's witnessed my giant fail. Look, I know you were punishing me, but it's fine – whatever.' She turned to Lucy and Hermione. 'Anyway, I also wanted to say that I'm sorry about SummerTube and the date clash. It's just that this competition is a huge deal for Anya as well as me, and I can't let her down. She can't do it without me.'

There was a delighted cackle behind her. She snapped her head around and saw Dakota high-fiving Kayleigh.

'Can I help you?' Jessie asked impatiently.

'No, no,' said Dakota sweetly. 'Please carry on with your fascinating discussion . . . You've actually just helped me win a fiver from Kayleigh.'

'What are you talking about?' asked Hermione.

Kayleigh smirked. 'When we saw that lame "What's in My Gym Bag" video, Queen Dee bet me a fiver that

Jessie wasn't going to be making many more videos for your channel.'

'What?' growled Jessie. Since when did they think it was acceptable to trade bets about her?!

'It's nothing personal,' said Dakota smugly, 'but when I saw you talking about your smelly leotards with your pathetic little gymnast friend, I just had this feeling . . . and it sounds like I was right. Not turning up for your big moment on the farm and now missing SummerTube? Not good, Jessie. Not good.' She took some vanilla perfume from her bag and spritzed herself happily.

Jessie felt her blood pressure rising. As always when Dakota gave her a hard time, her mind boiled over with ideas for pranks she could play on the self-satisfied bully. She remembered a video Jake had shown her recently of a group of school kids who hired a mariachi band to follow their teacher around on the last day of term. The teacher had found it funny, but she could almost taste Dakota's reaction to three men in giant sombreros playing loud music on their guitars and trumpet, giving her cheesy grins as they followed her from class, to class, to her locker . . .

She tuned out of her fantasy as she realized that Lucy was having a go at Dakota.

'Not that it's any of your b-business,' Lucy was saying with surprising fierceness, 'but Jess isn't l-leaving the channel. We're just talking about ONE event that sh-she can't make.'

Dakota looked bored. 'OK, if you say so, Lucy Lockjaw. But I know that five pounds is coming to me one day.'

'Good for you,' said Hermione as the bell rang. 'And a little tip – maybe have a good look at your own channel before you pass around criticism. I nearly fell asleep during your last video.'

Hermione flinched as Kayleigh took a step towards her in retaliation, but Dakota took her friend's arm and they walked off. *Even their backs look smug*, thought Jessie.

'Ugh, they are SUCH losers,' she said. 'And that vanilla

perfume makes me want to gag. I'm gonna get her good with a prank one of these days . . . I can't believe she implied I should quit the channel!'

Abby glanced at her. 'So . . . you're definitely not?'

'What? No! Of course not!' said Jessie, rolling her eyes. 'Come on, Abs. You're being ridiculous.'

'It's just that . . . we need another person to stand in for you at SummerTube,' said Abby, 'and if we find someone good, it makes sense to keep that relationship going.'

Jess couldn't work out if Abby was still punishing her, or if she really meant it. 'As in, you'd want them to join the channel? Permanently?'

Abby shrugged. 'Yeah, maybe. It would be a way of guaranteeing more content.'

Jessie had always believed in 'the more the merrier', but the thought of being replaced after months of making videos with the group was seriously painful. More painful than when she'd sprained her wrist dismounting from the parallel bars a few years ago.

'But it d-doesn't mean you can't stay too,' said Lucy quickly. 'It's just that we all have other commitments, so it makes sense to get a bigger gang together.'

'Yeah, and it's only going to happen if we find someone good,' Hermione added. 'It's no big deal, but we're going to meet up with SassySays, like we were planning to anyway.'

There was an uncomfortable pause as Jessie digested this news.

'OK, I have to run,' said Hermione. 'Let's speak later.'

Hermione and Lucy rushed off abruptly, and Jessie was left staring at Abby.

'Wow, that was awkward,' said Jessie. 'So you've obviously all discussed this without me?'

Abby folded her arms. 'The world doesn't revolve around you, Jessie, and we had to do something to make sure there would be four of us on the panel. It was for the good of the club.'

'I get it,' said Jessie, her mouth dry, 'of course I do. But you didn't have to leave me out of the discussion.

I'm still part of the team, and I still want to make videos. Like the cooking one I'm doing later with my family.' She could feel her voice wavering. 'Just because a couple of things have gone wrong recently, doesn't mean I'm not committed.'

Abby shrugged. 'If you say so. Anyway – I have to get to class. We can talk about it later.'

Jessie's day proceeded to get worse. After school, when she and Anya ran through their routine for Laila, she was dismayed to find her confidence from yesterday had evaporated.

'Sorry!' she said halfway through the routine, drawing a complete blank and coming to a standstill. 'What comes next again?'

Anya stared at her in horror. 'Are you kidding? It's the cartwheel into a full twist – you know that!'

Jessie nodded tiredly as it came back to her, her muscles aching.

'Maybe Jessie needs a little more practice,' said Laila gently. 'Why don't I give you two some time to polish this – I'll be back in twenty minutes.'

'No! We know it, we know it,' insisted Anya. 'I promise, Laila – we did it perfectly yesterday. Tell her, Jess!' She glared fiercely at Jessie with her clear blue eyes.

Jessie gulped. 'Yeah, sorry, I just had a moment . . .' Her head pounded and she suddenly felt like she didn't want to be there. But there was nowhere to hide. She took a deep breath. 'Let's try again.'

When the same thing happened a second time, and Laila had left them on their own, she turned apologetically to Anya. 'I've had a rough day; my brain is a pile of rubbish right now. I think I need a break. Do you mind if we finish early today?' She also wanted the time to prepare for her cooking video with Dad, but she decided not to mention that bit.

Anya folded her arms. 'You rushed off yesterday too,' she said suspiciously.

'I know – I had some filming to get to,' said Jessie. She

sighed. 'I ended up missing it, actually. It was awful.'

But she soon realized she wasn't going to get any sympathy from her partner.

'Jess, you need to focus on your gymnastics and this routine! And we need Laila's notes today so we can practise more!' As she jogged on the spot, Anya began listing the reasons they needed to focus, to win gold, or at least a medal, and Jessie groaned inwardly as the words trickled past her.

All she could think was, *However hard I try, I can't please anyone!*

VLOG 8

14:32

FADE IN: JESSIE'S KITCHEN.

DAD is in an apron stirring pans on cooker, and JESSIE is cutting up salad on kitchen island.

JESSIE

Hi, guys! So tonight we're having a special family

dinner – for once, the whole family will actually be here.

Anyway, this is my dad   say hi, Dad!

DAD turns to camera, smiles and waves a wooden spoon.

JESSIE (CONTINUED)

Tonight we're making tacos . . . my favourite! I've been running
around all day and I am FAMISHED. Talk us through it, Dad.

DAD

So, Jess, I'm frying up the meat
and I've got the beans cooking
too. The tortillas are warming
in the oven. How are we doing
on the rest?

JESSIE

I've chopped up the lettuce, onions and tomatoes, and now
I've just got to grate the cheese.

LEON and JAKE enter kitchen.

LEON

Hey, when's dinner? I'm starved!

DAD

Soon, Leon. You can help by laying the table. Also, can you put

out the guacamole, sour cream and chilli sauce?

LEON starts setting out plates, etc.

LEON

Do we have any real chillies? That shop sauce isn't hot

enough . . .

DAD

Actually, we've got quite a few: jalapeños, cayenne peppers, Scotch bonnets. I got them for trying out some more Mexican dishes.

JESSIE

OK, Leon. Later we can do the Chilli Challenge! Show us what you're made of!

FADE TO: The whole family sitting round table: DAD, MUM, LEON, JAKE and JESSIE, MAX in his high chair.

MUM

So I thought that was a brilliant dinner – especially since I didn't have to cook it!

JESSIE

Yeah, Dad. Maybe you should become a chef . . .

DAD

Nooo, I think I'd rather keep it as a hobby.

LEON flexes his biceps for the camera.

LEON

So who's up for the chilli challenge?

JESSIE

Me!

JAKE

Me! What about you, Mum?

MUM

OK, sure!

LEON

So I've been watching these chilli
challenges on YouTube . . . The world's
hottest chillies are the Carolina Reaper
and the ghost chilli. They both rate over a
million on the Scoville scale of hotness.

15 000 000
3 000 000
1 000 000
600 000
300 000
100 000
50 000
30 000
10 000
5000
1000
0

JESSIE

Wow! I didn't even know there was a scale for that . . .

LEON

People eating the Carolina Reaper sometimes have asthma

attacks, puke or even get taken to hospital!

JAKE

Awesome!

JESSIE

OK, so what's the drill?

LEON

We line up the chillies in order of hotness and then . . . we

just have to eat them.

JESSIE

Do we get to drink water?

DAD

Actually, water doesn't help with
chillies; you need milk.

LEON

Yeh, but if you drink the milk,
you're out! Ready?

MUM

Can we all be careful . . . I don't want any of us to get sick!

LEON

First the jalapeños . . .

LEON, JESSIE, MUM and JAKE all pick up a chilli and start
chewing.

LEON (CONTINUED)
Down the hatch!

JESSIE

(chewing)

Spicy, but not too bad . . . All done!

JAKE

Me too! Next one?

LEON

So this is the serrano . . . looks the same, a little green chilli,

but much hotter . . .

JESSIE

Mmm. Delicious!

JAKE

Help! My throat's starting to burn . . . not sure how much

more I can take. Owww!

LEON

Don't be such a baby . . . Mum?

MUM

No problem . . . you forget I grew up on curries and hot

pepper sauce!

JESSIE

So next we're on to this lovely red cayenne pepper . . .

(munching)

OMG this is A LOT hotter! OWW my mouth!

JAKE spits out the cayenne pepper.

JAKE

My mouth is on fire! Help! I quit!

LEON

You wuss! Leave it to the champ!

JESSIE

Ha! We'll see about that!

JESSIE waves her hand in front of mouth to cool herself.

MUM

(laughing)

Vamanos!

DAD

I think Mum could be a serious contender here . . .

LEON

So here's the Scotch bonnet . . . It's about ten times hotter

than the last one!

JESSIE

Easy!

(she starts chewing)

Not too bad . . . oh . . . wait . . . my whole mouth and throat

is on fire . . . now my stomach . . . aaargh!

LEON

Youch!

LEON starts slapping his knees and stamping his feet.

LEON (CONTINUED)

I didn't think anything could be this bad!

LEON jumps up and down, tears streaming down his face.

JESSIE

AYYY! I can't do this any more! Pass me the milk!

JESSIE spits out the chilli pepper and starts swigging the milk.

DAD

That was impressive, Jess – but you were sensible to quit!

Leon?

LEON

I've done it! I've done it! . . . OMG – that was the

worst thing ever . . .

MUM picks up another Scotch bonnet pepper.

MUM

OK, Leon, here's the real challenge . . . Can you eat

a second one?

LEON

Whaat??! No!!!! Not fair!

JESSIE

Ha ha ha! Go, Mum!! Leon, she's gonna win!

LEON is sulking and drinking his milk.

LEON

That wasn't what we agreed . . .

MUM finishes chewing the chilli and fist pumps to signal victory. Then drinks her glass of milk.

JESSIE

Result! Girls rule! Hashtag *Hot Mamma*!

DAD

Literally! Well done, honey . . . and all of you! How about some ice cream?

JESSIE

Brilliant!

(to camera)

So guys, thanks for joining my family for dinner and the chilli challenge. Let me know if you'd like us to do any more family challenges in the comments down below, and give us a thumbs-up if you enjoyed this vlog! Byee!

FADE OUT.

Views: 4,982

Subscribers: 16,434

Comments:

HashtagHermione: I can't believe your mother did that!! Slaay!

foodchallengeking: Easy – I can do five Scotch bonnets, no lie 😄

PrankingsteinJosh: Hahaha, Leon's face at the end!

billythekid: RIP, your taste buds.

StephSaysHi: I can't bear spicy food

AlwaysFelicity: Your family is fun xx

funnyinternetperson54: Props to your mum, those things are nasty!

peter_pranks: Did anyone else think Leon was going to vom? Ha ha!

(scroll down for 12 more comments)

Chapter
Nine

On Saturday morning Jessie, stuffed full of pancakes, sprawled on the sofa in the living room flicking through the comments on her chilli vlog. Her mouth still felt sore from the peppers, but it had been so much fun to film with her family, and she was proud of the result.

'Can I see?' asked her mum, sitting next to her.

'Sure!' she said. 'We got lots of views, which is great!'

They replayed the video, snorting with laughter at the moment where tears started streaming down Leon's face.

'That was fun,' said Jessie's mum. 'We don't get enough

time together as a family. Anyway, how **are** you doing, sweetie? Everything OK? You seem a bit stressed . . .'

'No, I'm OK, Mum . . . just a lot on my plate . . .'

Jessie was tempted to crack and tell her mother everything, but she felt if she started talking, she might burst into tears, so she said nothing.

When her mum had left, Jessie caught up on Dakota's latest video, entitled 'PROM: EXCITING REVEAL!!' Even though she was still furious with the way Dakota had belittled her last week, she was mildly curious to see what the big news was. It turned out that Dakota's parents were hiring a posh limo and chauffeur to transport her to the prom, and she was looking for ten 'lucky viewers' to go with her.

'Guys, I've seen the car and it's pimped out. To. The. Max,' Dakota announced proudly, smoothing her hair and grinning into the camera. 'Trust me – I'm talking chic leather interiors, mood lighting, state-of-the-art entertainment system . . .'

You're a state-of-the-art pain in the neck, thought Jessie.

She couldn't believe Dakota's cheek, using yet another treat from her parents to win herself extra popularity. Every school friend who followed her channel and posted a comment would be entered into a prize draw to win a place in the limo, Dakota promised. The worst thing is, it was working: loads of the boys had commented as well as girls, clearly impressed by her bragging about the limo. Even Eric, who Jessie knew for a fact found Dakota unbearable.

As she started to rewatch the video despite herself, Jessie's phone pinged with a group message from Abby.

10:34

> **Abby:** I've invited Sassy to my house tomorrow! You all have to come! xox

Jessie sat up straight, instantly forgetting about Dakota's video. That hadn't taken long to arrange . . . and she wasn't sure how she felt about it.

First she decided not to go. Then she remembered

that she had told Abby that she wanted to be involved with group decisions, so it would look really bad if she wasn't there. Besides, she was actually quite curious to see what the chatty Sassy was like in real life.

But she was still angry with Abby, and she still had an uncomfortable, jealous feeling about Sassy that she couldn't shift. What if everyone liked her better? What if she was louder, funnier, more outrageous . . . and became best friends with all the others? What if they realized that everything was better without Jessie around to mess it up?

'LOOK OUT!!!' screamed Max, charging into the living room and swatting at her ankles with his glow-in-the-dark light sabre.

'Maxy!' she cried.

'You're dead!' he said proudly, swatting harder.

She giggled. 'I'm gonna get you, Maxy!'

Her spirits lifted and as she chased her energetic little brother up and down the stairs, a feeling of determination took hold of her. She'd been a part of

GCV since the beginning, and she wasn't going to allow anyone to elbow her out.

She messaged the group a few moments later:

10:58

Jessie: I'll be there. Can't wait.

'Hi,' said Abby coolly, opening the front door to let Jessie in.

'Hi,' said Jessie. *Still awkward*, she thought. *Definitely still awkward.*

'Hermione can't come until later – she's being forced to meet her dad's new nightmare family. But Lucy's in the kitchen with Mum, and Sassy should be here any second. She lives forty minutes away and her dad's driving her.'

'OK,' said Jessie, unsure of what else to say. She grabbed Weenie who was yapping loudly, relieved to have a distraction.

'Do you want a dr—'

They were interrupted by Josh running out of the door. 'Hi, Jess! Just heading out to meet Charlie – see you guys later!'

Jessie waved at Abby's brother, noticing Abby shudder slightly at the sound of Charlie's name. Then she heard a voice saying, 'I think this is it, Dad,' behind her. She turned to see a girl with two pink mermaid plaits walking up the driveway, accompanied by a tall, burly man. Jessie waved at Sassy – that hair was a definite giveaway.

'Hi! Sassy, right? I'm Jessie.'

'Yes!' The girl grinned. 'I know – I recognize you from taco night! And this must be the famous Weenie.'

Sassy's father looked at Jessie suspiciously. 'I thought you hadn't met any of them yet,' he said to his daughter. 'When did you go out for tacos?'

Sassy blushed slightly. 'I'm talking about a video she made, Dad. That's how I recognize her. Weenie's the dog.' She looked into the open doorway where Abby was waving frantically. 'Oh, and you're Abby – hi!'

Soon they were all gathered inside with Abby's mum

and Lucy. Jessie soon figured out that Sassy's father wasn't as unfriendly as he'd first seemed. He was just worried about his daughter meeting people off the internet. Which was fair enough, she thought . . . her dad would have acted in exactly the same way.

'Where's the fourth one?' Sassy's father asked at one point, looking around.

'Hermione can't make it just now,' explained Abby. 'She might come over later.'

'Is she another school friend?' he asked, his forehead creasing in concern. 'How old is she?'

Jessie tried not to laugh at the thought of the sweet and mild-mannered Hermione somehow being the untrustworthy one of the group.

'Fourteen – and I promise she's a very positive influence on these girls,' said Mrs Pinkerton reassuringly. 'A bookworm *and* an excellent baker! I do understand your worries, especially as this is Saskia's first time meeting people from the internet. But these girls really do support and look out for each other –'

at this, Jessie couldn't help but raise an eyebrow at Abby, who pretended not to see – 'and all of us parents stay in touch to make sure everything's going well with the Girls Can Vlog channel.'

Jessie tried to sneak a proper look at Sassy. She seemed a bit more shy than she appeared in her videos, but that was normal. And it was always embarrassing hearing your parents ask questions on your behalf.

Later, when Sassy's father seemed satisfied that everything was OK, and nobody wanted to kidnap his daughter, he announced he'd be back to collect her in a couple of hours, and the girls went upstairs to Abby's bedroom, followed by Weenie.

'Sorry about that,' said Sassy at once, settling herself down on one of the beanbags. 'Totally cringe!'

Jessie grinned. As she'd predicted, the girl was immediately coming out of her shell now that they were alone. 'Parents!' she said sympathetically, wrestling with Weenie over his favourite chew toy.

'They're all the s-same,' added Lucy. 'I guess it's good

they're l-looking out for us . . . and

I suppose the internet had barely been invented when they were our age, so it's no wonder they're suspicious.'

'Ha ha, true! Your room is so cool, Abby,' said Sassy. She took in the spacious white room, decorated with fairy lights and pretty furnishings. 'I can see why you film so many GCV videos in here.'

'Thanks! I've started putting a lot more work into making it nice, now that I know it's not just for me, but for the viewers too.'

For the viewers too, mimicked Jessie in her head. When had Abby become so annoying?

Abby glanced around. 'I actually tidied this morning because we were thinking of making a video later. Do you want to join in?'

'Definitely, as long as I can borrow some lipstick!' Sassy puckered up her lips. 'I don't feel the same vlogging without it. Just call me Miranda Sings!'

'Lipstick? I d-don't think Abby owns any of that . . .' joked Lucy.

Missing the sarcasm, Abby gestured to her amazing make-up cabinet and pulled out a drawer, which had been entirely given over to lipsticks and glosses. 'It's all yours, Sassy.'

'Thanks!' said Sassy, looking through the red shades. 'By the way, I've never collabed with anyone before, so apologies if I suck.'

'I m-might borrow some too.' Lucy also started rummaging through the drawer. 'You'll b-be amazing, Sassy.'

'Totally – and I've got the perfect idea for a challenge we could do.' Abby checked her phone. 'Hermione says she can make it in an hour, so we can include her – great.' Her tone had become businesslike. 'Let's talk about SummerTube first. So, Sassy, you're definitely up for coming with us? Like I said in my message –' she glanced at Jessie – 'RedVelvet entered us as a group of four for the panel, and now we've got a spare space.'

Jessie felt her cheeks burn.

Sassy raised an eyebrow. 'Are you kidding? OF COURSE. I've never been to a big convention before, and being on a panel with you guys would be incredible!'

'Excellent,' said Lucy. 'We w-were so worried about l-losing our place, and you feel l-like such a good fit.'

Abby looked thrilled. 'I'll tell RedVelvet you're on-board. This has worked out perfectly!'

Jessie stared at the floor, but nobody noticed how quiet she was being.

'Obviously my dad will have to OK it,' chattered Sassy, 'and he'll have a hundred million questions, but apart from that it should be a done deal. He knows how much YouTube means to me. So, do we really get our hotel room paid for?'

Jessie felt a surge of jealousy wash over her as Abby explained more and the feeling of excitement in the room grew stronger. She carried on playing with Weenie, trying not to look as miserable as she felt.

'Was it you that couldn't make it, Jess?' asked Sassy eventually.

There was a pause.

'Yeah,' she mumbled. 'I've got a stupid clash with my gym competition and unfortunately I can't do both. It's really annoying.'

'Oh yeah, I saw your "What's in My Gym Bag" video – so cool! It's sad you can't make it, but you must be so talented if you're in a competition. I'm the least sporty person ever,' said Sassy mournfully. 'Can you do the splits?'

'Sure,' said Jessie. 'Shall I show you?'

She ignored Abby, who was rolling her eyes, and went into the front splits. Sassy cheered and then begged her to do some backflips in the corridor outside, which she did with pleasure, loving that Abby was so annoyed by the distraction.

Once Hermione had arrived, Abby started talking them through the video they were about to film.

'Wait – before we get into that, can we go over a few ideas for pranking Dakota at the prom?' Jessie asked, suddenly finding her voice. 'I've decided it's got to happen!'

Abby sighed irritably. 'I don't know if now is the best time to—'

'Yes! Great idea,' squealed Hermione. 'She's become unbearable, even by her standards. Have you guys seen that limo video? Ridiculous.'

'Sassy, Dakota is this impossible p-person in our year who has been bullying people for ages,' explained Lucy. 'Including me for my s-stammer. On top of that, she's now become the w-world's biggest show-off on her YouTube channel.'

'Showing off how?' asked Sassy, intrigued. 'Wait – is she the one who did that chicken nugget thing with Prankingstein? The girl in the red dress?'

Jessie nodded. 'Yeah, that's her.'

'That was pretty uncomfortable to watch,' said Sassy. 'She was trying so hard to look cool while getting sick to her stomach. Not good.'

Weenie whined loudly, as if in agreement, and they all laughed.

'She'll do anything for attention,' said Jessie. 'She's head of the prom committee and she keeps giving out "tips" on YouTube for how to make the best of the night, but it's all just a front to remind us how amazing HER night is going to be.'

'She's just announced that her parents are hiring this incredible limo, and she's lording it over everyone and trying to make us all "win" places in the limo with her. I mean *please*!' said Hermione. 'She's forgotten she's an actual school kid – she honestly thinks she's a celebrity.'

'Wow,' said Sassy, trying on a cherry-red lipstick. 'It sounds like a prom prank is exactly what she needs . . .' Her eyes roamed about the room. 'A limo, you say? We could work with that . . . !'

'Funny you should say that. Great minds . . .' Jessie's eyes lit up as she showed Sassy the list of ideas that she'd scribbled down on the bus journey over. She pointed to her favourite one, which she'd circled several times over.

DAKOTA PROM REVENGE

Steal her shoes.

Ruin her dress.

Feed her toffee onion disguised as toffee apple.

Hijack limo and kidnap Dakota!!!! ☺ (in my dreams . . .)

Cling film

VLOG 9

What Am I Touching? Collab with SassySays

12:48

FADE IN: ABBY'S ROOM.

LUCY, ABBY, HERMIONE, JESSIE and SASSY sitting cross-legged on the floor near a large tray covered in a tea towel.

ABBY

Hi, everyone! Look – we have Sassy from the amazing SassySays doing a collab with us today!

ABBY gestures at SASSY, who takes a bow.

ABBY (CONTINUED)

If you don't already know her, you should subscribe to her

channel – I'll leave the link below.

SASSY

(waving)

Hi, GCV fans! I'm so excited to be here, though a little freaked

out about what the guys have in store for me.

JESSIE points at the tray and does her best evil laugh.

HERMIONE

I'd be worried too . . .

LUCY

It's n-not that bad! Today we are playing the 'What Am I

Touching?' challenge, and we thought it would be f-fun for our

guest to be the guesser! We're going to p-present Sassy with a series of objects, and she'll have to g-guess what each one is by touch alone!

JESSIE

OK, Sassy, no turning back now – it's blindfold time!

JESSIE and ABBY take a scarf and wrap it around her eyes.

SASSY

Help! I can't see a thing!

ABBY

Excellent – so let's get started.

ABBY removes the tea towel from the tray and picks up a tiny cactus in a pot.

ABBY (CONTINUED)

We've each chosen an object from around the house –
here's mine.

ABBY hands it carefully to SASSY, who grabs it enthusiastically,
then drops it.

SASSY

OWW! That hurt!

They all wince in sympathy.

LUCY

Abs, that was mean!

ABBY

(apologetically)

Oops! I wasn't expecting her to pick up the whole thing! Sorry!
But . . . can you guess?

SASSY blows on her fingers.

SASSY

A load of needles?!

ARRY

Kind of . . . I'll give you a clue, as I feel guilty for injuring you! I have a few of these on my windowsill.

SASSY

(grinning)

A cactus!

LUCY

Correct! And now mine, which m-might help with the pain.

From out of shot, she picks up WEENIE and holds out one of his ears to SASSY.

LUCY (CONTINUED)

H-here.

(mouths to the camera)

Stop wiggling, Weenie!

SASSY

Ha ha, this is very soft and velvety. And, it smells like dog!

Weenie, is this your ear?!

LUCY puts him down.

LUCY

Yes, well d-done!

HERMIONE

Trust you to choose an animal! OK, here's mine, Sassy . . .

ready?

HERMIONE pulls out a bowl of
cake mix with a spoon in it from
the tray, and carefully hands it
over to SASSY.

SASSY

Ooh, this is heavy!

SASSY feels around the edges of the bowl, then sticks her hand right in it. They all laugh.

SASSY (CONTINUED)

(shaking her hand)

Argh, cold! What is this stuff . . . yogurt?

HERMIONE

You can try some if you like . . . Here's a spoon.

HERMIONE hands it to her. SASSY cautiously tastes a tiny bit.

SASSY

Yum! I'm going to say . . . cake mix? Lemon flavour!

HERMIONE

(clapping)

Very good! I'll need to take it back downstairs before Abby's mum realizes it's missing.

LUCY nudges HERMIONE.

LUCY

T-trust you to choose a baking thing!

JESSIE

And finally, mine! Put your hands out.

JESSIE drops a plastic bottle of pink glitter glue into SASSY's hands.

SASSY

This feels like make-up, maybe?

JESSIE

Nope!

SASSY

Ooh, eye drops?

JESSIE

Nope!

SASSY

OK, let me see if I can open it.

SASSY unscrews the lid and squirts the glue into her open palms.

SASSY (CONTINUED)

Ew! This feels sticky.

SASSY rubs her palms together.

HERMIONE

I wouldn't do that if I were you . . .

SASSY

Er, I can't pull apart my hands! This must be glue!

JESSIE

(jumping up)

Correct! Ding ding ding! And for a bonus point,

what kind of glue?

LUCY

Hint: we're at Abby's h-house.

SASSY

Erm, sparkly glue! Glitter glue!

JESSIE

And the colour?

SASSY

Pink?

ABBY

Correct!! To match your hair! Well done and thank you for

being such a good sport. You can remove the blindfold now.

SASSY gingerly lifts up the scarf, laughing.

SASSY

That was gross! I'd like to wash my hands now please!

(to camera)

I had no idea what I was getting myself into,

hanging out with these girls! Comment below if

you think I should do the challenge back

to them . . .

LUCY, HERMIONE, JESSIE AND ABBY

Please no!! Byeeeee!

FADE OUT.

Views: 7,090

Subscribers: 17,010

Comments:

StephSaysHi: Ahhh YES! I love Sassy – all my faves together 😍

PrankingsteinJosh: The cactus was always going to end badly, LOL.

queen_dakota: Recruiting another saddo to boost the failing channel? Lame.

ShyGirl1: You guys make a great team x

pink_sparkles: She should definitely do the challenge back to you. Ha ha!

miavlogs: Loved this xox

(scroll down to see 43 more comments)

Chapter Ten

One week later . . .

7:45

Jessie: I CAN COME!!

8:02

Abby: ??

8:03

Jessie: To SummerTube! My comp changed dates to this w/e.

Abby: Are you sure?

8:04

Jessie: Yes! But is it a problem with Sassy? Please say I can still come? 😜

8:20

Abby: Not sure, let me check . . .

Jessie checked her sports kit one last time, nervously humming 'What a Feeling' from *Flashdance*, the song to which she and Anya would be performing their routine. Leotard, scrunchie, hairbrush, hairspray, make-up, deodorant – check. Manicure, a last-minute treat from her mum for training so hard – check. It was the first one she'd ever had and she was in love with the intricate pink-and-turquoise arrow pattern, which looked as professional as the designs worn by Olympic gymnasts and matched her leotard. She was touched that her mum had treated her when she knew that money was tight at the moment.

'You can do this,' she muttered to herself, chewing a gummy worm and trying to calm her jittery nerves. The competition had moved forward by a week due to a mix-up with the venue, which meant she and Anya had had less time to prepare. She was filled with adrenaline at the last-minute nature of it, but they'd fitted in extra practice sessions, and now she just wanted to get it over with.

And of course she was glad that it had moved, because it meant that hopefully she could still attend SummerTube. Well, she would definitely attend as a visitor, but RedVelvet still had to confirm whether she could be on the panel as well as Sassy. Jessie had agreed with the others that it would be mean to disinvite Sassy at this late stage, so she had to hope for the best. Abby was still being weird with her, but she couldn't worry about that today.

Jessie heard a honking outside the window and saw

Anya's mum's car awaiting her. She grabbed her bag and ran down to the kitchen.

'Say goodbye to Jessie,' her father told Max in his high chair, who gave her a big wet kiss on the nose.

'Thanks, Maxy!' she cried. 'See you guys later!'

Her family would be driving to the competition separately. *Just as well*, she thought – Leon and Jake were still half asleep at the breakfast table, and may or may not have grunted a 'good luck', it was impossible to tell.

She jumped into the back seat of the car. 'Hi, guys!'

'Hello, Jessie! I hope you're feeling good today,' said Anya's mum. 'I was just giving Anya some last-minute tips.'

Jessie had met the ex-gymnast a few times now, and she was a kind, well-meaning woman, but within seconds her strict advice was making Jessie's nerves soar even higher.

'Remember – the judges will be scrutinizing every tiny movement. Even when you're standing still, they will examine you for posture, focus and concentration, so you must never relax and forget yourself.'

They were all things Jessie had heard before from Laila, and Anya herself, but they weren't helping her now. 'It's my first inter-club competition, so my main aim is to get through it alive,' she joked.

Nobody laughed, and Jessie realized that her comment had gone down like a lead balloon.

'Of course I'll do my very best, though,' she added hastily, 'for Anya's sake as well as my own.'

'You'll be great,' said Anya confidently. 'We both will.'

Jessie grimaced. 'Hope so!'

'Do you know anyone else who is competing?' asked Anya's mother.

'No – we're the only ones from our club, so we've got no idea,' said Jessie. 'I think Laila said there are ten other pairs in our category.'

As they pulled into the car park, she noticed a few other competitors arriving, including a pair of identical twins with tightly woven plaits swinging down their backs. They had expensive-looking tracksuits on and were deep in conversation, their heads bowed together.

'They look . . . serious,' Jessie said nervously. 'I wonder if they're under-fifteens too.' Then she told herself that she didn't care about placing higher than other people or winning a medal. She was just in it for the experience, and to improve. But deep down she couldn't help hoping . . . after all that practising, it would be so amazing to walk away with a prize! Jessie had never trained for anything so hard in her entire life.

After they'd registered and said goodbye to Anya's mum, who went to find a good seat in the arena, they headed for their allocated changing room. They weren't on for another hour, so after getting changed they took the time to stretch and walk themselves through their routine once last time.

Next, Jessie did her hair and make-up (a slightly toned-down version of the look Abby had done for her, and not quite as perfect), did Anya's eyeshadow for her in matching turquoise, then checked her phone. Lucy and

Hermione had sent her cute messages, and she wished they could be there – but with the last-minute change of date, they hadn't had time to organize anything.

Laila arrived and shepherded them towards the main hall. 'Looking fantastic, girls!' she said proudly. 'Love the make-up. So, the time has come! Break a leg out there – or, you know, don't . . .'

Jessie rolled her eyes at the corny joke, wiping her sweaty palms against her legs as they entered the huge, echoey stadium. It was the largest space she'd ever performed in. They found some seats on the rows of tiered benches, which had been reserved for the competitors, and she looked down at the equipment laid out in the centre of the room: the pommel horse, the parallel bars, the balance beam. Judges, competitors and coaches milled around and the air was thick with a sense of excitement and anticipation.

After an introduction from the lead judge for her category, the first pair took to the floor.

'Remember, you're up fourth,' whispered Laila as the

music started blaring. 'A nice place to be: not first, and not too long to wait around getting nervous.'

'Too late – I'm already nervous,' said Anya.

Jessie looked at her in surprise. *'Really?'* It was the first time her partner had ever displayed an ounce of uncertainty – she was the most confident gymnast Jessie had ever met!

'It's good to be a little nervous,' Anya replied, shrugging, as if it was all part of the plan. 'Keeps your mind sharp.'

'That's true,' agreed Laila. 'You can channel those nerves into energy once you're out there. Hey, is that your family, Jessie?' She pointed to where Jessie's mum, dad and all three of her brothers were sitting in a row. Maxy and Jake were waving ferociously at her – obviously Leon was acting too cool to join in.

'Ha, that's them all right,' said Jessie, feeling much better for seeing them and waving back. 'Embarrassing! And there's your mum next to them, Anya. Cute!'

Fifteen minutes flew by far too quickly, with some

impressive performances from the first competitors. The twins Jessie had seen earlier were the clear front runners. They were amazing to look at in their silver-spangled leotards, their performances perfectly in sync as they cartwheeled diagonally across the mat to Katy Perry's 'Roar', exact mirror images of each other. It was like watching a single gymnast through double vision.

The scores had been a mixed bag, with the twins taking the lead. *There's no way we're beating them*, thought Jessie, but she stopped herself from saying anything to Anya.

'OK, you're up,' said Laila, escorting them down to the floor mat they would be performing on. 'Remember – you've got this!'

Suddenly Jessie's heart was in her throat. She looked up quickly at her family, then gasped. Was that . . . Lucy . . . sitting next to Leon? And Hermione taking her place beside her. They'd made it after all! The panicky, jangly feeling went away as she was overcome with happiness at seeing them. She looked up again to see if Abby was there too – she wasn't.

No big deal, Jessie thought as she stepped on to the mat, trying to ignore the little stab of disappointment.

She assumed her starting position, one arm in the air and one toe pointed. As the first notes of their song blared out loudly over the speakers, she looked into Anya's eyes and gave a tiny nod. They could do this. Next she calmly, confidently established eye contact with the judges – and began.

Several flips, handstands, cartwheels and a lot of choreography later, it was over. It had been a complete blur! She couldn't really tell how it had gone, but there was loads of applause ringing in her ears as they saluted the judges, so it couldn't have been that bad – and she'd pulled off the aerial cartwheel perfectly. She hugged Anya and Laila, who came running over to congratulate them, then waved up at her support group. Only then did she notice that the girls were holding up an enormous banner that read 'GO JESS!' Maxy was cheering his little heart out, waving his light sabre triumphantly, and even Leon looked proud.

She held Anya's hand as they waited for the judges to mark them. The system was complicated as there were two different scores combined: the D score (difficulty of routine); and the E score (execution). So far the incredible twins had scored 15, but anything as low as 11 was an acceptable score. Anya squeezed her hand as a score was finally held up: 13.4.

Second place! But it wasn't over yet. There were seven more acts to go, so they'd have to sit patiently. Jessie tried not to gnaw at her newly manicured nails as she watched the other routines unfold. Everyone was of a good standard, none were perfect – everyone made the tiniest mistakes here and there. Their score stayed in second place until the tenth act – a meticulously performed routine by two graceful and athletic Japanese girls, which stole their spot with a score of 14.2.

'We're still in with a chance for bronze,' breathed Anya. 'Just one to go.'

Silently they watched as the final pair took to the floor. Like them, these two were mismatched in height. They started off confidently, but when the shorter gymnast had to climb on to the bent thighs of her tall partner, she failed to get her footing, and they had to abandon the move.

'That will cost them,' whispered Anya, but Jessie still couldn't speak.

The pair finished off their routine neatly, with an impressive couple of backflips and plenty of applause. And then it was time for the scores: 12.3.

'That means . . . that means . . . we're third!' cried Jessie, eyes wide. 'Is that right, Laila?'

Their coach punched the air. 'Yes! Which makes you bronze-medal winners in your first ever competition together. Well done, you talented things!'

Jessie and Anya hugged each other, jumping up and down, then congratulated the other finalists.

As the prize podium was set up, Lucy came running over followed by the others, still carrying the banner.

'Have you won? Have you won?!' she cried. 'I c-couldn't work out the scores, but I saw you celebrating.'

'Third place!' said Jessie. 'Bronze!'

'Amazing!' cheered Lucy, flapping the banner in their faces. 'You looked so p-professional out there. I c-can't believe how good you both are.'

'We took a zillion photos,' added Hermione. 'I actually think I might have a second calling as a sports photographer.'

Jessie grinned as her family and Anya's mum came and joined them too. She felt on top of the world and couldn't wait to get up on that podium to accept her medal.

'Next time, with a bit of work, it will be silver – or gold,' said Anya's mum firmly.

'With *a bit of work*?' said Jessie, remembering the hours of her life that had led to this wonderful moment. 'Ha ha ha ha!'

VLOG 10

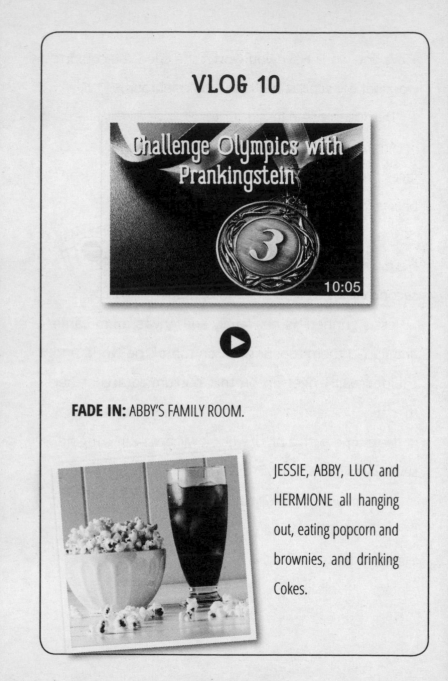

FADE IN: ABBY'S FAMILY ROOM.

JESSIE, ABBY, LUCY and HERMIONE all hanging out, eating popcorn and brownies, and drinking Cokes.

HERMIONE

Hi, guys! So we're all here celebrating the fabulous Jessie and her bronze medal at the under-fifteens competition yesterday.

LUCY

We're so p-proud of you. You and Anya were amazing!

HERMIONE

I couldn't believe the backflips. All that practice really paid off.

JESSIE

Jeez, thanks, guys! Your support means everything to me. I didn't think you'd be able to make it.

LUCY

Let's have a l-look at your medal.

HERMIONE and LUCY admire the medal as JESSIE passes it round. ABBY, back turned, very busy sorting out things on the counter so doesn't join in.

ABBY

(irritated)

Guys! Can we please focus on today's vlog?

(to camera)

So, hi! Today we've got a really fun vlog planned with the

Prankingstein boys: the Challenge Olympics.

HERMIONE

And Jessie gets to be the judge!

JESSIE

Ooh, power at last! Where are the teams? Come on boys, out

you come.

JOSH and CHARLIE enter.

CHARLIE

Hey! It's the champ!

CHARLIE and JESSIE high-five.

CHARLIE (CONTINUED)

What've you got in store for us?

JESSIE

So we've got two teams:
Charlie and Abby; and Josh
and Lucy. Hermione's offered
to do the time-keeping. There
will be three challenges:
Eating M&Ms with chopsticks;
popping the most balloons
in the fastest time; and the
Chubby Bunny Challenge.
Let's go!

HERMIONE

So for the first challenge you have to eat M&Ms using
chopsticks, one hand behind your back. There's one hundred
M&Ms on each plate; how many can you pick up and eat in a
minute? Ready?

ABBY

Ooh, I love M&Ms – should be easy.

CHARLIE

I'm not very good with
chopsticks . . .

HERMIONE

One, two, three – GO!

ABBY, CHARLIE, LUCY and JOSH all start shovelling in M&Ms as
fast as they can.

JESSIE

Abby's doing well. Lucy too . . . Josh, you're pretty useless!
Keep trying, Charlie!

HERMIONE

Thirty seconds left.

JESSIE

No cheating, Josh! You can't just hoover them up with your
mouth! You need to use the chopsticks.

HERMIONE

Ten seconds.

JOSH picks up the plate and pours the M&Ms into his mouth.

JESSIE

JOSH! You've just disqualified your team. Abby and Charlie won
that round.

ABBY

Yay!

ABBY gives CHARLIE a friendly punch.

ABBY (CONTINUED)

We're a winning team!

JOSH

Glad to see you two are on good terms again, not!

(to Lucy)

Sorry, Luce. I'll do better next round.

HERMIONE

So Abby managed to eat forty-two M&Ms,

and Charlie ate thirteen.

JESSIE

OK, this next challenge is
to pop fifty balloons in the
fastest time. The record is
eight seconds. You can't use
anything except your bodies.

HERMIONE

So here we have two bunches of fifty balloons, which took

FOREVER to blow up . . . I'll start the countdown . . .

JOSH whispers to LUCY

LUCY

Yup, g-got it!

HERMIONE

One, two, three – GO!

ABBY and CHARLIE start stamping on the balloons, but JOSH and LUCY throw themselves lengthwise down on the balloons, popping a lot in one fell swoop.

LUCY

(shouting)

Ouch! I really b-bashed my knee . . .

JESSIE

Great start there, guys. Clever technique.

ABBY

Help! They keep getting away from me . . . Charlie! You've

gotta do something!

HERMIONE

Twenty seconds left and still lots of balloons.

JOSH

One more time . . .

JOSH hurls himself on to remaining balloons.

JOSH (CONTINUED)

Lucy, just stamp on the ones round the sides.

JESSIE

Lucy, Josh, you're doing great . . . just a few more . . .

LUCY sits down on the last balloon, which pops loudly.

HERMIONE

That's it! That was just over a minute.

JESSIE

Lucy and Josh are the winners of round two! Charlie, Abby, not your finest hour . . .

CHARLIE

That was harder than I thought it would be. They're slippery little things. Sorry, Abs.

ABBY

Never mind – we can still win. What's next?

JESSIE

It's the Chubby Bunny Challenge where you have to stuff as many marshmallows as you can into your mouth and say 'Chubby Bunny' after

each one. The team that's eaten the most and still can

speak is the winner!

CHARLIE

Luckily I love marshmallows . . .

JESSIE

Ready, steady, GO!

MONTAGE: Fast-forward of all four contestants stuffing marshmallows into their mouths and saying 'Chubby Bunny' less and less coherently, now all with cheeks bulging.

LUCY

Ugh-ugh-ugh-ugh . . .

HERMIONE

I couldn't really understand that, I'm afraid.

JESSIE

Lucy and Josh, you are now out. If Charlie and Abby can
manage one more each, they'll be the winners of this round
and the competition.

CHARLIE squashes one more marshmallow in.

CHARLIE

Chu-y . . . Unny!

ABBY looks desperate, waving her arms as a marshmallow half
sticks out of her mouth.

ABBY

Chu- chu- . . .

CHARLIE

C'mon, Abs!

CHARLIE taps ABBY's nose affectionately.

CHARLIE (CONTINUED)

Be my Chubby Bunny!

ABBY makes a huge effort and shoves rest of marshmallow in.

ABBY

Chu-y Bunny!

JESSIE

(shouts)

Yay, we have a winner! It's 'Chabby'!

ABBY and CHARLIE smile at each other triumphantly and do a fist bump.

FADE OUT.

Views: 9,304

Subscribers: 18,430

Comments:

MagicMorgan: Woohoo, the return of Chabby!

PrankingsteinCharlie: It was just our team name :)

StalkerGurl: I'd do 'Chubby Bunnies' with you any day, Josh.

StephSaysHi: Loved thIs!

GabsDoesGym: Congratulations on your bronze medal, Jessie!

girlscanvlogfan: *Runs to the shop to buy M&Ms*

SassySays: I need to meet these Prankingstein boys.

queen_dakota: How soppy! Made me almost vom . . .

Amazing_Abby_xxx: That wouldn't take much!

(scroll down to see 53 more comments)

Chapter Eleven

'How is it *today* already!' said Hermione as they ate their lunch in one of the playing fields. Friday had arrived, and it was a warm, sunny day, and they couldn't wait to get out of school. 'Can you believe we're going to SummerTube in just a few hours?'

'You have mentioned it a few million times, yes,' said Dakota, sunbathing nearby in a vest top and with her skirt rolled up.

'A few billion, you mean,' Ameeka said with a smirk, rubbing sun cream into Dakota's back.

But the girls were too excited to rise to the bait. 'I don't know how I'm g-going to concentrate on afternoon lessons,' said Lucy, passing around her crisps. 'I c-can't believe it's really happening!'

Dakota sighed loudly. 'Honestly, overreact, much? It's not like you're the only people going to SummerTube,' she said mockingly. 'You missed a bit, Meek. There, no, by my shoulder. SHOUL-DER. Yeah, my dad got me a VIP ticket, so I'll be there too, with my vlogging camera. And isn't your dumb brother going with Charlie, Abby?'

'Yes, he is, but there's one key difference,' said Abby triumphantly. 'You're all going because you're paying to be there as *visitors*, VIP or otherwise. WE are going there as GUESTS of RedVelvet and to CONTRIBUTE to a panel on fresh talent. All expenses paid. Because of our popular, inspirational, award-winning channel.'

Hermione looked uncomfortable. 'It hasn't technically won any awards, Abs,' she said.

Jessie felt uncomfortable for another reason. She still wasn't completely sure whether the five of them were going to be on the panel, even though RedVelvet had agreed to pay for all five girls' travel and hotel room. It would be weird for her to go and not be able to take part.

'Did you get a chance to ask about the panel, Abs?' she asked quietly. 'When you talked to Tiffany yesterday?'

'Ask what?' said Abby.

Jessie sighed with irritation. Why was Abby being so mean? 'You know, if it's OK for all five of us to do it.'

'Oh that.' Abby sniffed. 'I didn't want to bother her. We can ask her on the train, but they are pretty strict on numbers.'

'F-fingers crossed,' said Lucy, smiling at Jessie.

A few hours later, Jessie, Hermione, Lucy, Abby and Sassy sped through the countryside on a train bound for London. They had settled into their first-class carriage with Tiffany, dressed in a trademark cherry-red jumpsuit, and Paul, her manager, who spent most of the journey glued to three different phones.

There had been a commotion at the station, with several RedVelvet fans spotting Tiffany and begging her for selfies, Abby running late ('I couldn't decide what to pack!' she'd cried, brandishing not one, not two, but *three* suitcases), and Sassy's father asking Paul a hundred questions about the arrangements for the weekend. It was a miracle that they'd made the train on time, but now the stress had evaporated and Jessie was trying to find the right moment to ask about the panel.

Initially she'd felt nervous at seeing Tiffany after her no-show at the Springdale City Farm shoot – she knew that the YouTuber had probably found it unprofessional. But Tiffany put her at ease as soon as the train left the station by saying, 'I heard you did amazingly in your competition, Jessie – way to go!'

And Jessie wasn't the only nervous one – Sassy was slightly overwhelmed at meeting Tiffany for the first time.

'I feel like I'm dreaming,' she told her. 'I mean, I've been watching your channel since I was nine, and here I am just casually catching the train with you.'

Tiffany laughed. 'I can imagine it's the weirdest thing.'

She passed her one of Hermione's home-made white-chocolate brownies. 'You'll get used to it though; these four have! I've watched your channel too, by the way. You're a great addition to the team.'

'So what happens once we get there?' asked Abby, who had Tiffany's adorable bichon frise, Bambi, nestled in her lap.

Jessie waited anxiously as Tiffany sipped her coffee and glanced at the schedule on her phone. 'So, we arrive in about an hour, get picked up by a couple of cars and taken to the hotel. We'll check in, have some dinner – maybe go for burgers, or room service, it's up to you – then try to get our beauty sleep before the big day.' She stretched her legs out. 'I for one am going to have a nice bath and a face mask. It's been a long week.'

'Yeah, and I'll need some time to look through my outfits,' said Abby. 'Plus we might do a teensy bit of filming in the hotel.'

Worries about the panel aside, Jessie couldn't wait to see the hotel. She'd looked at it online, and she and the girls were sharing two big rooms with a connecting door. The double beds were enormous, and the TVs looked like cinema screens.

'I may have packed my karaoke machine too . . .' said Sassy suggestively.

'You have a k-karaoke machine? Amazing!' cried Lucy.

'You guys should definitely relax and enjoy yourselves tonight,' said Paul, glancing up from his phones. 'But don't stay up too late. Tomorrow, we'll have breakfast at the hotel and then get taken to the convention, where we have the morning free to walk around. We need to have you all ready for the panel by 2 p.m.'

'Er, on that note,' said Jessie tentatively. 'Is it definitely OK for me to be part of the panel – for us to be a five, rather than a four?'

Tiffany looked at her in surprise. 'Sure, they were fine with it. I texted Abby last week to let her know.' She smiled at Jessie. 'Why else would you be on this train with us?'

Jessie gasped, then noticed both Lucy and Hermione

look accusingly at Abby – it was obvious she'd decided not to pass on the message. It was almost as if she didn't want Jessie to come at all.

'Didn't I tell you, Jess?' Abby said carelessly. 'I thought I had.'

After taking a second to process the deception, Jessie decided to rise above it. For now, anyway. 'Oh, maybe you did,' she said, equally carelessly. 'I was just checking.'

Her relief at being allowed on the panel meant that she was happy to ignore Abby for the time being. But her mind set to worrying about the event instead. She knew the others had been preparing for it while she'd been at gym practice, and now it suddenly occurred to her that she might not be ready.

Despite the tension between Jessie and Abby – which everyone pretended didn't exist, though Jessie could tell Sassy was confused – the girls had a brilliant, hyper night in the hotel. They stayed up until 1 a.m., against

Paul's advice, singing, ordering room service, vlogging, and getting to know Sassy.

The next afternoon they arrived early at the exhibition centre where the convention was being held. Jessie spotted the enormous neon-orange SummerTube posters and immediately felt a thousand times more nervous than she had arriving at the gymnastics competition. Hundreds of people were swarming around the entrance, and she squealed as she caught glimpses of YouTubers she recognized – including the beautiful and hilarious Cinnamon Buns (real name Amelia), Tiffany's friend, who came over and took selfies with them all.

Paul gave them lanyards to wear around their necks, which they proudly flashed at the entrance guards. Then he had to escort Tiffany off to a book signing on the other side of the hall.

'I'll come and find you girls later,' he said. 'In the meantime – you have my number.'

'Have fun – make sure you explore everything!' Tiffany

waved before being engulfed in a crowd of fans through which Paul steered her with determination.

It felt weird being left on their own.

'How does my outfit look?' Jessie asked Lucy anxiously. 'Is it kinda over the top?' She'd deliberately chosen clothes to stand out from the crowd, but suddenly she panicked that she looked like an idiot.

'No you look incredible, t-trust me. Those leopard-print leggings are awesome,' said Lucy admiringly. Then she looked at something behind Jessie's shoulder. 'Oh my god, Abby – there's Josh and Charlie!'

Abby stared for a second, then took out her lipstick. 'I didn't think they would get here so early. Here, hold this up for me.' She shoved a mirror into Lucy's hand.

Hermione spoke up. 'Looks like Charlie brought Louise.'

Abby stopped in her tracks, her lipstick half done. 'What?' She glanced over. 'I assumed they were – well, he was just so flirty the other day when we were filming . . .' Her face stiffened. 'I'm going over,' she announced.

'Are you sure? There's s-so much to see here,' said Lucy. 'Do you really want to spend time with those guys – it m-might bring you down?'

Abby shrugged. 'It's fine. Catch up with you in a bit.'

They all watched as Abby walked over and hugged both her brother and Charlie, then greeted Louise with a cool wave. Jessie cringed – this was going to be awkward.

'What's the deal with those two?' asked Sassy. 'Chabby, I mean.'

'Trust me – your guess is as good as ours!' said Hermione, rolling her eyes. 'It's a never-ending mystery.'

'And we're all bored to death of it,' said Jessie loudly. 'So let's stop talking about it and go and explore!'

She was officially done with Abby's nonsense. Her heart raced with excitement as she looked around at the massive hall, with people coming and going, vlog cameras and selfie sticks out in force. Whatever Abby thought, Jessie belonged here.

*

'Guys . . . I'm not doing this,' said Abby as they sat around a table backstage, five minutes before they were due to take their places on the Fresh Talent panel. She got to her feet.

Now what? thought Jessie. 'What do you mean?' she asked impatiently. She was fizzing with excitement as she looked around at the other YouTubers making their way on to the stage, and she didn't want Abby to ruin her buzz.

'Yeah,' said Hermione anxiously. 'What are you talking about, Abs?'

Abby fanned herself with her notes. 'The panel. I'm not ready. None of us are.'

Sassy's eyes widened with alarm. 'Huh? Is it because I'm new?'

'Well – there's that, let's be honest,' said Abby, her voice wavering. 'Plus the fact that Hermione is super shy, Lucy stutters, Jessie messes stuff up all the time, and I – I am just very worried! About how unprofessional we might look to our fans! I'm getting out of here.'

'HEY!' said Jessie, outraged. How could Abby put them all down like this? She called after Abby as the girl left the room, striding furiously after her into the corridor. 'I can't believe *you're* chickening out of this, after all you put *me* through for being late to the photoshoot! How is THAT professional, Abby, huh?'

Then she caught sight of Abby's sweaty forehead and pale face. She'd obviously worked herself up into a complete state and was having what looked like the beginnings of a panic attack. 'Hey, we'll be fine,' she said more softly. 'Take a few deep breaths, that helps me with my gym nerves. In for five, and out for five. In for five, and out for five.'

Abby crouched down in the corridor and followed the instructions. 'Can you believe Charlie is here with that drip Louise?' she said miserably after a few breaths.

'Don't think about that,' said Jessie. 'Today is about you – about us – and we are going to be amazing. Come on, this is our big moment!' She took Abby by the hand

and led her back into the room, where the others looked over anxiously.

'Where's Tiffany?' Hermione looked around. 'Guess we need to tell her if we're pulling out.'

'M-maybe this *was* a bit ambitious,' added Lucy. 'We can always come back next year.'

'Abby's fine, and we're not going anywhere!' said Jessie, banging her fist on the table. The others jumped. 'We are SO ready, I promise you. Look at how far we've come, in such a short time. Look how many subscribers we have. Why d'you think Tiffany invited us in the first place?'

Abby looked at her. 'Maybe . . . she couldn't find anyone else?'

Jessie laughed. 'That's ridiculous, even for you, Abs. You of all people know how well we're doing – and no, it hasn't been the smoothest journey recently – but nothing in life is! We won't get this kind of opportunity again; we've got to just go for it.'

'But what if we make idiots of ourselves? Do you know

how many people are going to be filming this?' Abby said.

'Yes, a lot! Which is amazing for us! We'll get loads more subscribers,' said Jessie.

'Jessie's right,' said Hermione slowly. 'We need to believe in ourselves, even if this is pushing us out of our comfort zone.'

'That's true,' agreed Lucy. 'I m-mean, pushing myself out of my comfort zone is the r-reason I got started on YouTube in the first place, so w-why stop now?'

'EXACTLY!' said Jessie triumphantly.

Sassy looked confused. 'Wait. So we ARE doing the panel?' Abby took a few loud breaths in and out, then smiled weakly at Jessie. 'Yes, we are. Thanks, Jess. You talked me down from my moment of madness.'

Jessie grinned and smiled at her friend. 'We're all good, then?'

'We're all good. Though I probably owe you an

apology.' Abby looked shyly at her. 'I know I've been pretty terrible to you lately.' Suddenly, her businesslike expression took over. 'But we can deal with that later – there's no time to chat. Places, people!'

VLOG 11

Our Fresh Talent Panel at SummerTube!! — Feat. SassySays and RedVelvet

11:33

FADE IN: HOTEL ROOM.

HERMIONE filming herself in the mirror in the bathroom of the hotel room, in pink cupcake PJs and fluffy rabbit slippers.

HERMIONE

Hi, guys! We're here in our AMAZING hotel because tomorrow we are speaking on a panel at SummerTube. I still can't believe it – I feel so nervous. Tonight we are lucky enough to chill out here – not bad, huh! Here's a mini room tour for you . . .

The camera pans around the room. We see ABBY flinging clothes around, LUCY on the sofa devouring an enormous sundae and waving at the camera, JESSIE and SASSY jumping on the bed having a pillow fight.

It pans back to HERMIONE.

HERMIONE (CONTINUED)

As you can see, some of us need to wind down a bit before tomorrow . . . We'll see you at the convention!!

CUT TO: SUMMERTURF PANEL.

Camera pans to see a large
room filled with teenagers
seated in rows. The camera
zooms in to the table at
the front where the panel
of twenty are answering

questions, and then zooms in further to TIFFANY and the Girls
Can Vlog crew.

AUDIENCE MEMBER #1

I'd like to ask Lucy and the others from Girls Can Vlog, did you
ever think you would get this far in under a year? You're at
almost twenty thousand subscribers and already
speaking on a panel!

LUCY

(laughing)

I h-had no idea. I started my little channel j-just as a way to work on my confidence. I expected to h-have about two subscribers – my mom and my dad! But as soon as these g-guys joined in, things happened so quickly. And Tiffany's support has been really important too.

ABBY

Definitely! We just messed around in the beginning, but for the last few months we've made more of an effort to produce regular content, which does seem to have paid off.

JESSIE

Even if that's really hard work and sometimes you'd rather chill out in front of Netflix rather than film another video!

The crowd laughs as JESSIE pulls a face.

JESSIE (CONTINUED)

But the comments and feedback we get mean it's totally worth it. We love entertaining people.

TIFFANY

This is why these guys represent the best of YouTube fresh
talent to me. They're great role models because even when
things aren't easy, they persevere! And they're honest, too,
showing their fans all sides of their lives, even when things
aren't perfect.

AUDIENCE MEMBER #2

(rude voice)

If they're doing so great, why is there a new one in the group?
Are the original four struggling?

HERMIONE

(looking out)

Ah, hi there, Dakota. Glad you could make our event.

JESSIE can be seen muttering 'Oh for God's sake!!'

ABBY

(professionally)

Great question. We're really happy to have Sassy joining in on some of our videos. We felt she brought a new dimension to Girls Can Vlog, and of course she brings lots of fans from her own channel. It just means we can guarantee even more content and variety!

The crowd applauds.

SASSY

I've been a fan of these girls for months and it's been incredible getting to know them. We have so many hilarious treats lined up for you!

AUDIENCE MEMBER #3

If you need a sixth member, I'm free!

The crowd laughs.

ABBY

We'll bear it in mind, thanks!

The camera pans out over the crowd.

HERMIONE

(voiceover)

So that was a sneak peak of our big panel, hope you enjoyed

it! Thanks to Josh for filming our big moment – we're still on

cloud nine. See you soon!

FADE OUT.

Views: 30,203

Subscribers: 19,399

Comments:

MagicMorgan: You killed it! So proud. ❤️❤️❤️

maggiemay: I'm the one who volunteered to join!! Still available!

CinnamonBuns: So great meeting you guys xxxxx

sami_rules: You were my favourites on that panel.

miavlogs: I'm getting my hair dyed like yours Sassy ❤️

queen_dakota: For more sophisticated, inspiring content, please check out my channel . . .

Sammylovesbooks: Did you meet any other booktubers, Hermione?

HashtagHermione: Yes, so many – SummerTube is amazing for meeting people with similar interests

Amazing_Abby_xxx: Erm, Dakota – can you stop trolling for followers on our channel!?

(scroll down for 249 more comments)

Chapter
Twelve

It was tough going back to school on Monday after the frenzied excitement of the weekend.

'Who needs GCSEs anyway?' Jessie asked her father, who was busy feeding Max, as she grabbed her lunch from the fridge.

'You do,' he replied, without missing a beat. 'Don't forget to take an apple from the fruit bowl.'

Jessie selected the shiniest one and put it in her bag. 'Not being big-headed, Dad,' she continued, 'but we are basically YouTube personalities now, and besides that I have the makings of a very promising gymnast.' She stared dreamily into space. 'Jeez, just think of the opportunities ahead of me!'

Her father roared with laughter, causing Max to do the same. 'Not being big-headed, you say?'

'Nope, simply stating facts.' She grinned. She knew she was exaggerating, but this was fun . . . and she thought there was at least some truth in what she was saying. 'I just don't think I need physics in my life any more.'

'Well, stick with it for the moment, Miss Big Opportunity, and we can talk about it again in a couple of years' time. For now, trust an old man when he says having an education seems to work out well for most people.'

'If you say so,' Jessie said with a sigh. She sidled over to the kitchen counter and took the cling film out of a drawer.

'What are you doing with that?' asked her father.

'Nothing – just . . . a science project. You know, education!' she improvised hastily, shoving it in her rucksack 'Oh, and if you go shopping, I might need a second roll too.'

At school Hermione met Jessie in the car park and handed her three rolls of cling film. 'We always have loads at home, for my baking,' she explained.

'Yessss! I need as much as I can get,' said Jessie. 'Thanks.'

'And remind me what this is for, exactly?' asked Hermione, raising a suspicious eyebrow.

Jessie knew that they'd forgotten the discussion about pranking Dakota, and had decided to keep quiet about it for maximum effect at the prom.

'I told you, all will become clear!' Jessie grinned. 'Clear as this cling film, in fact, ha ha! See you in registration – I've just got something else to sort out.'

Hermione shrugged. 'Good to see you're still one hundred per cent certifiably insane,' she called as she walked into the school building.

Next Jessie went to the bike shed, where Charlie and

Josh were waiting for her as planned. She'd managed to talk to them in private at SummerTube, towards the end of the day, and they were fully onboard to help her execute her plan.

'How's it going?' asked Charlie.

'I'm collecting the supplies,' she said, 'hoping to get twelve rolls by the end of the week. Is that enough?'

Josh nodded. 'Should be. When we did it with the furniture at my dad's office, we only got through ten, and that included five computers.'

'Brilliant. And, Josh, you're still on standby to distract *you know who* for half an hour on Friday while Charlie helps me do the deed, aren't you?'

For best results the prank needed to be executed quickly and simply, with minimum fuss.

'Definitely,' said Josh. 'Oh, there's my mate. I've got to run, but text me if you have any more questions.' He ran off.

 Charlie smiled at Jessie. 'I can't wait for Operation Cling Film – this is going to liven up that stupid prom no end,' he said gratefully. He kicked at a bike tyre. 'Don't know if I'd even bother going, otherwise.'

Jessie looked at him curiously. 'Are you bringing Louise?'

'I guess so.' Charlie sighed. 'The thing with Louise is . . . at SummerTube—'

'Oh no, did Abby say something to her?' asked Jessie. Abby hadn't told them what had happened, and while she felt a bit disloyal talking to Charlie about their conversation, she was desperate to know.

'Abby was just Abby,' said Charlie with a smile. 'As always! No, that wasn't a problem. The thing is, Louise met these people at the exhibition . . .' He stopped and ran his fingers through his hair.

'OK?' prompted Jessie. 'She met some people?'

'Yeah.' He looked down. 'Warhammer enthusiasts.'

'Warhammer? As in that game with all the miniature figurines?'

Charlie nodded. 'That's the one. So they had a stand for Warhammer strategy games on YouTube?

It's this whole thing. Louise spent ages talking to them, and now she's obsessed. She was messaging me all day yesterday while she was watching, like, a million Warhammer videos.' He sighed. 'I knew she had a geeky side to her, and I thought it was kind of cute at first, even if she was a bit too obsessed with *Lord of the Rings*, but this is another level. She wants me to get involved, and she's ordered loads of the kit.' He frowned. 'I just don't get it and I don't think we have that much in common.'

'But that's cool, if she's found a new hobby!' said Jessie. 'Isn't it?' She tried not to laugh at the slightly alarmed look on Charlie's face.

'I guess,' he said uncertainly. 'It's just – Warhammer? With all those elves and wizards? I'm not sure.'

The bell rang for registration and they parted ways.

'Don't freak out,' called Jessie. 'It'll all be fine. See you Friday!' *Fascinating*, she thought. *But I won't say anything to Abby just yet.*

*

On Friday the girls got ready at Abby's house after school, then Mrs Pinkerton drove them back to school for the prom at 7 p.m. 'Enjoy yourselves, ladies!' she cried as they got out of the car. 'You look a million dollars!' She'd insisted on taking dozens of posed photos of them in the living room, which Jessie had found slightly awkward, but now that she was here she could only think about her prank.

Hordes of people were arriving, and two teachers – Miss Piercy and Mr Byrne – were on hand to chaperone the students. Mr Byrne looked resplendent in a tuxedo and polka-dot bow tie, which Miss Piercy was adjusting for him. He smiled down at her, blushing beet red.

'Those two!' said Hermione. 'Adorable!'

Sam arrived and presented Lucy with a beautiful corsage with a pale pink rose. She squealed. 'How h-handsome does my boyfriend look?' She wasn't usually big on public displays of affection, and Jessie made gagging noises until Lucy knocked her over the head with her clutch bag.

Jessie's excitement grew as they entered the main hall, which was already pulsing with loud music and decorated with flashing lights. She noticed Kayleigh and Ameeka manning the food and drinks table and immediately regretted not making the toffee onions that would have livened things up from the start. Although one prank was probably enough . . .

'Hi! Did you come with Dakota in the famous limo?' she asked casually, helping herself to a cupcake.

'No, she hasn't arrived yet. She offered the places to some of her new subscribers,' said Kayleigh, turning a bit pink. 'But, whatever. We were happy to make our own way, weren't we Meeks?' she said defensively.

Ameeka stirred the punch miserably. 'Of course, it's not a big deal. We totally get that she needs to grow her social media support base. We just got the bus.'

Kayleigh glanced irritably at Jessie. 'If you've finished, some other people might want to get to the snacks now?'

'Wow,' Jessie muttered to Hermione as they went

to join the others. 'She didn't even let her best friends ride with her. I actually feel sorry for them – no wonder they're always in a terrible mood.'

'It's unbelievable,' said Hermione, shaking her head. 'Why people continue to stick around with her is a mystery to me.'

Suddenly there was a very loud thumping noise from the school entrance, drowning out the music in the hall.

'What on earth?' said Mr Byrne, hurrying out, followed by most of the prom-goers.

'I think her royal highness has arrived,' said Abby, as a sleek white vehicle pulled into view.

Lucy sighed. 'Let's g-get this over with.'

'Yes.' Jessie giggled. 'Let's see what the big fuss is about.'

As they all gathered by the entrance, the limo pulled to a stop outside. An immaculately dressed chauffeur stepped out of the driving seat, then opened a back door. Dakota, wearing a sequinned silver gown and some sky-high silver stilettos, slowly stepped out, delicately taking the chauffeur's gloved hand. She was followed by a group of Year Nines, none of whom Jessie had ever seen hanging around with Dakota before, all cheering and clinking glasses. Music blared out from the back seat, and the party atmosphere was obvious. Despite herself she felt a brief flash of envy.

'WOOOHOOO! Let the fun commence!' shouted one of the boys, to large cheers from the crowd.

'Dakota, you look amazing,' screamed someone.

She nodded graciously.

'. . . And that ride is off the hook!'

Jessie had a quick look inside the back of the limo while she could.

'You want a ride in it later?' murmured Dakota, noticing her interest. 'Make it worth my while and I'll think about it.' She raised her voice, flicking her perfectly waved brown hair. 'That goes for the rest of you. Places on offer for those who deserve one. I'll make my selection at the end of the night . . . At the other end, there'll be an after-party at my house for the lucky few.'

Sam frowned in confusion. 'Is she, like, asking for bribes or what?'

Lucy giggled. 'Who knows. Welcome to the weird world of D-Dakota. But there's no way any of us are getting in that l-limo.'

'No way *anyone* is,' Jessie muttered to herself, grinning.

They went back into the hall and started dancing. Interestingly Charlie had arrived alone.

'Louise stayed home . . . with her new miniature friends,' he explained when Jessie asked. 'It's probably for the best. We had . . . a chat . . . so things are a bit awkward now. Anyway, are you all set?' He smiled secretively. 'Three hours to go.'

Everyone was hot from dancing and excited to see the band had come on for their second act.

'The driver's gone to get a drink – it's time!' said Charlie, rushing up to Jessie and hissing in her ear. 'Josh is waiting outside. I'll meet you there.'

Jessie looked at him. 'Jeez, already? OK, back

in a sec.' She slipped out of the hall, avoiding the questioning glances of her friends. She ran up the stairs and into the darkened corridor where her locker was, using the torch on her phone to light her way.

Collecting the rolls of cling film, she dashed back down the stairs, dropping them as she went. *Take a breath!* she reminded herself, picking them up again and trying to contain her excitement.

Then she slipped through the hall towards the back of the dancers, and outside. The limo was still in the car park, and she spotted the chauffeur talking to Josh a few metres away. Charlie was crouched down by the front wheels. He put his finger to his lips, and she crept over, her heart racing . . .

'So that's Eric, Pia, Evie, Beyoncé, wait hang on . . .'

The prom had finished and Dakota was shrieking excitedly to the crowds following her out of the hall, as Jessie peeked out from behind the bike shed holding her breath. Jessie had gathered the girls and Sam, plus Josh and Charlie, with her.

Dakota became even more high pitched. 'Actually not you, Beyoncé. Beatrice, Sarah-Ann, Freddie, Justin – come on, guys!' she trilled. 'Kayleigh and Meek – I'll see you at mine. If you get there first, put the drinks on ice, would you?'

'Please, Dakota!' cried a desperate voice. 'I've never been in a limo.'

She tutted as she glanced at the hapless guy. 'As if, I'm not a charity. Tom, are you coming? OK, how many is that? Finally, what about –' She broke off, and her jaw dropped open. There was a gasp from the onlookers.

Jessie continued to hold her breath as the prom princess stared at the sight in front of her. 'What the– ?'

'OOOH, SHAME!!!' cried the unlucky contender in delight. 'Looks like you're not going in a limo either!'

Jessie silently high-fived her friends as their faces lit up. Covered from bumper to bumper in tightly wrapped cling film, Dakota's beautiful chariot now looked like a super-sized sandwich left in the back of somebody's fridge. Dakota tottered up in her silver stilettos and tried one of the door handles, but they were completely coated in the strong plastic.

'What on –? I'm calling Daddy!' she shrieked, her face puce with fury. 'This is outrageous! Where's the chauffeur? He wasn't meant to leave the car.'

'I hope he won't lose his job,' whispered Hermione, as the driver arrived at the car park and covered his mouth, trying not to laugh at the scene in front of him.

'It's cool,' said Josh. 'He told me this was his last shift – he's becoming a landscape gardener.'

'Who can b-blame him?' said Lucy. 'Oh my g-god, this is hilarious.'

Dakota was trying to unwrap the cling film with her manicured fingers, but she only removed a few shreds before giving up and shrieking in annoyance. Jessie noticed Kayleigh approach, about to help, before Ameeka grabbed her by the arm and held her back.

'Guess the after-party's off then,' said Jessie.

As Dakota stomped back into school, Jessie gathered the others to help her undo the damage. Apart from Charlie and Abby, who stayed behind the bike shed, chatting intently and looking into each other's eyes . . .

VLOG 12

FADE IN: THE PARK.

LUCY, ABBY, HERMIONE, JESSIE and SASSY are all in shorts and T-shirts on a picnic blanket in the park, sipping brightly coloured smoothies.

LUCY

Hi, everyone! Isn't the weather g-glorious?! Who wants a sip of my delicious B-Berry Bonanza?

JESSIE

I'm happy with my Mango Madness, thanks!

(to camera)

So, you've all been sending us your questions to our Girls Can Vlog Instagram. Let's do a random scroll through. We posted a picture of us at SummerTube, and because we didn't get a chance to answer everyone's questions on the day, we thought this would be a great opportunity to answer a few more. So, Hermione, take it away!

HERMIONE

OK, so to start off with, LoveKelly asks, 'Is there any kind of video you haven't filmed yet that you want to?'

ABBY

Ooh, good one!

(thinks)

I'd like to do a 'Get Ready With Me' – can't believe I haven't done that yet.

JESSIE

More group challenges – there are so many options out there!

SASSY

Same! I'm still getting used to filming with other people and it's

so much fun, even if it's harder to edit!

LUCY

Interview with my c-cat!

JESSIE looks at her in surprise.

LUCY (CONTINUED)

Look it up; it's a thing!

HERMIONE

If you say so, Luce. I'd like to interview an author one day . . .

as in a real human, ha ha! OK, next up – flowerpower45 says,

'What are your goals for the channel?'

LUCY

We'd love to do more t-travel
vlogs, if we get the chance. Let us
know if you like them as m-much
as we like making them in the
comments below.

ABBY

Agree! It was amazing vlogging our ski trip and also our time at
SummerTube.

JESSIE

Yeah, now we just need to find something exciting to film in
the holidays.

SASSY

Pleeeease!

HERMIONE

LibbyJessica asks, 'Are you all single?'

LUCY

Nope!

(looks around)

Well I'm not! Anyone else w-want to comment?!

SASSY AND HERMIONE

Not really . . .

JESSIE

I'm single and ready to mingle, wooh! Abby? You've

gone a bit quiet.

ABBY awkwardly sips her smoothie.

ABBY

Next question!

Everyone giggles.

HERMIONE

One for Jessie from ItsChloe, 'Do you prefer
gymnastics or YouTube?'

They all look at JESSIE.

JESSIE

Oh, man! Why do I have to pick one? Both!!

ABBY

Cop-out!

JESSIE sticks her tongue out at her.

HERMIONE

Finally, Weenie_for_president wants
to know, 'What have you learned from
SummerTube and is Sassy staying on
as the new member?'

LUCY, HERMIONE, ABBY and JESSIE hug SASSY.

JESSIE
We love her sooo much and she's definitely going to be
cropping up in a lot more of our videos!

ABBY
And to answer the first question, this is going to sound so
cheesy, but I learned that we work best as a team.

ABBY looks at JESSIE.

ABBY (CONTINUED)
Doing SummerTube showed me that we make
each other shine!

JESSIE

(grinning)

That was SO cheesy! But SO true. One last time – group hug!!

Byeee from us all and see you soon!

They all hug and fall over, laughing.

FADE OUT.

Views: 10,340

Subscribers: 20,496

Comments:

Amazing_Abby_xxx: OMG 20,000 subscribers – thank you everyone!!

RedVelvet: Congratulations girls, your hard work paid off x

violets_space: New subscriber here, my friend is obsessed with you guys ☺

miavlogs: Pretty please can you do a meet-up for your fans?

jazzyjessie: Great idea miavlogs, we'll think about it xox

girlscanvlogfan: YESSSSSS to a meet-up and more travel vlogs!!

animallover101: I would love to see Lucy interview her cat lol!

MagicMorgan: Has the queen lost her tongue?! Sad . . .

ShyGirl1: WHAT IS GOING ON WITH CHABBY???

(scroll down for 120 more comments)

Top Ten Tips:
So you wanna be
a YouTuber?

Anyone – thirteen years old or more – can become a YouTuber. All you really need is a camera (which could be your phone), a computer with an internet connection, and ideas! It really helps if you are a YouTube fan already – as this will give you inspiration on what to vlog about and tips on how to do it.

1) WATCH

Spend some time watching your fave YouTubers and take note of what they're vlogging about. What do you like about them? What makes you laugh and how do they inspire you?

What kind of vlogger do you want to be? Do you want to feature make-up and hairstyling? What about fashion and shopping hauls? Do you love gaming and want to film yourself competing online? Do you love pranks or challenges? Do you have a special talent like Jessie's love of gymnastics? Or maybe you'd like to try your hand at reviewing books, movies, games or music? All these and lots more are great topics for vlogging . . .

2) PREPARE

You shouldn't just turn on the camera and start filming . . . you need to prepare . . .

One hack is to use a notebook to help you brainstorm and record your ideas. Make lists about what you want to cover, what you need around you for your vlog and whose help you'll want to ask for.

3) DECIDE

So before you get started you need to establish your profile.

Decide on your username – try to think of something catchy and fun. To do this you could make lists of things you love or favourite nicknames. But first double-check that no one else is already using it.

4) DESIGN

Your own channel banner. Once again look at your favourite YouTubers for inspiration. You may be able to design your own or ask someone who's experienced at web design to help you. Remember to include your channel name in the banner!

5) READY . . .

First of all brainstorm ideas about what exactly you are going to do. Improvisation can be fun but only if you have an overall idea about what you are trying to show in your vlog.

Once you've decided on your subject, give your video a title. Plan your intro, the main content of your vlog and finally your sign-off. Having these signposts along the way will help keep you on track and give you some confidence. In the beginning it's a good idea to do a practice run without the camera running. If you think you might freeze while filming, have a few notes ready as reminders and stick them near the camera.

6) STEADY . . .

Check the background of where you are going to film! Is there enough light? Is it tidy or does it need decorating and styling with fairylights or something else? Is your background right for the subject of your video? Do you need any props: for cooking or a makeover? Make sure you have everything you need to hand.

Check your equipment and make sure it works: the camera or phone you are using, extra batteries, lights and microphone!

7) GO . . .

Be brave, switch on the camera and start talking. It really helps to have memorized your first sentence so you can launch right in. Be confident and keep smiling! Don't panic if you make a mistake as you can edit it out later!

We all love bloopers so make sure you laugh at yourself.

8) PAT

. . . yourself on the back when you've finished and go and have some chocolate! HOORAY!

9) EDIT

Editing is something that takes patience and practice. Don't despair; you will get better with each vlog. Your YouTube idols make it look easy, but they've been practising for years.

You will probably use the video-editing software that comes with your computer. Experiment with all the different effects you can get so you know what look you want to achieve.

You can make the vlog look like one long take, in which case you need to edit carefully so there is continuity. Or you could break the film up into scenes using special effects or text on the screen.

Then add your sound effects and music (but make

sure you have permission to use your music, or have used copyright-free material).

Don't forget to add links to the comments section on your finished video: subscribe to your channel, other useful channels or websites and your Instagram or Twitter links.

Show the rough-cut video to a friend or family member to make sure it's working. Take on board their comments but don't worry about making it perfect!

10) UPLOAD!

Once you have established a YouTube channel this should be very easy. There is information on YouTube about how to do this.

Choose a fun title which is descriptive. Add your thumbnail, which is very important for attracting viewers.

Add detail to the description box and tag using key words that relate to the video such as 'makeover', 'shopping haul' , 'prank' or 'Halloween' to help people who are searching for something particular find your video.

Upload, making sure the setting is private until you have double-checked everything. Then set to 'public' and share your YouTube stardom with the world!

Finally, always remember . . . **STAY SAFE ONLINE!** Ask your friends and family whether they are happy to be featured in videos BEFORE posting them. And NEVER EVER share your identity, address or the details of your school. Remember not to wear school uniform when filming, and be careful when vlogging in your garden if it's easily recognizable.

About the Author

Emma Moss loves books, cats and YouTube. In that order – though it's a close call. She is currently writing the next book in the Girls Can Vlog series.

HAVE YOU READ . . .

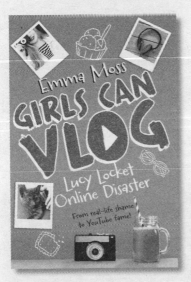

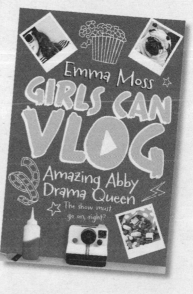